THE
INCENDIARIES

THE INCENDIARIES

R. O. KWON

virago

VIRAGO

First published in the United States in 2018 by Riverhead Books
First published in Great Britain in 2018 by Virago Press

1 3 5 7 9 10 8 6 4 2

A CIP catalogue record for this book
is available from the British Library.

ISBN 978-0-349-01187-5

Printed and bound in Great Britain by
Clays Ltd, Elcograf S.p.A.

Papers used by Virago are from well-managed forests
and other responsible sources.

Virago Press
An imprint of
Little, Brown Book Group
Carmelite House
50 Victoria Embankment
London EC4Y 0DZ

An Hachette UK Company
www.hachette.co.uk

www.virago.co.uk

To Clara Kwon and Young Kwon

이 책을 부모님께 바칩니다

At the bottom of everything there is the hallelujah.

—Clarice Lispector, *Água Viva*

THE INCENDIARIES

1.

WILL

They'd have gathered on a rooftop in Noxhurst to watch the explosion. Platt Hall, I think, eleven floors up: I know his ego, and he'd have picked the tallest point he could. So often, I've imagined how they felt, waiting. With six minutes left, the slant light of dusk reddened the high old spires of the college, the level gables of its surrounding town. They poured festive wine into big-bellied glasses. Hands shaking, they laughed. She would sit apart from this reveling group, cross-legged on the roof's west ledge. Three minutes to go, two, one.

The Phipps building fell. Smoke plumed, the breath of God. Silence followed, then the group's shouts of triumph. Wine glasses clashed together, flashing martial light. He sang the first bars of a Jejah psalm. Others soon joined in. Carillon bells chimed, distant birds blowing white, strewn, like dandelion tufts, an outsize wish. It must have been then that John Leal came to her side. In his bare feet, he closed his arm around her shoulders. She flinched, looking up at him. I can imagine how he'd have tightened his hold, telling her she'd done well, though before long, it would be time to act again, to do a little more—

But this is where I start having trouble, Phoebe. Buildings fell. People died. You once told me I hadn't even tried to understand. So, here I am, trying.

2.

JOHN LEAL

Once John Leal left Noxhurst, halfway through his last term of college, he drifted until he ended up in Yanji, China. In this city, adjacent to North Korea, he began working with an activist group that smuggled Korean refugees toward asylum in Seoul. He'd found his life's work, he thought.

Instead, he was kidnapped by North Korean agents, spirited across the border, and thrown into a prison camp outside of Pyongyang. In the stories he later told the group, he said the gulag brutalities were bad enough, but at least they'd been expected. What astonished him was the allegiance his fellow inmates showed toward the lunatic despot whose policies had installed them in their cells. They'd been jailed because, oh, they'd splashed a drop of tea on his newsprint portrait. A

neighbor claimed to have overheard them whistling a South
Korean pop song. Punished for absurdities, they still maintained
that the beloved sovereign, a divine being, couldn't be to blame.
At first, he assumed this was lip service, the prisoners afraid to
say otherwise. But then, he thought of the refugees he'd met in
Yanji, how they talked of loving the god they'd fled. They attributed the regime's troubles to anyone but the sole person in
charge.

A month into John Leal's time in the gulag, prison guards
held an optional foot race, the prize a framed icon of the despot.
In the confusion, those who fell were trampled. One child died
of a broken spine. Through howls of pain, he shouted hosannahs
for his lord. They weren't lying, the poor fools. They believed
in the man as one might believe in Jesus Christ. Some people
needed leading. In or out of the gulag, they craved faith. But
think if the tyrant had been as upright as his disciples trusted
him to be. The heights he'd have achieved, if he loved them—if,
John Leal thought, until his idea began.

3.

PHOEBE

I hoped I'd be a piano genius, Phoebe told the group, in the first Jejah confession she tried giving. She'd have sat in the circle, holding a kidskin journal. Though I'd driven Phoebe here, I was outside, going home. It's a mistake. I should have stayed, but I didn't. Instead, I'll add what details I can. The full lips, spit-polished. She licked them, tense. I'm striving to picture it: Phoebe, talking. The thin, long-fingered hands folded tight. She looked down, inhaled.

But I didn't just wait, she said. I expected, no, I wanted to work for it. I spilled time into the piano as I'd have put cash in a bank. I saw full concert halls in the future, solo recitals. Front-page plaudits. I practiced Liszt while imagined spotlights gilded the living room. Recollection is half invention, but it feels as though I spent my entire childhood training to prove I was the significant pianist I believed I'd be.

So, I piled up trophies. It wasn't enough. The teacher flicked my hands with a rod each time I didn't hit the right note, but I didn't mind. My ambition outstripped his. Let my hands swell. I could use the extra span. Bright-knuckled, I tried again. The months ticked past, then years. I kept lists of rivals; I indexed others' exploits by age. Kiehl, at five, had given his first recital to the Danish king. Ohri, eleven, debuted at Carnegie Hall; Liu, fifteen. One night, my teacher called Libich's Étude no. 5 the most challenging piece a soloist might attempt. It's eluded the finest pianists, he said. I rushed to find the étude's score. I learned it alone, in secret. I memorized Libich's high trills. I flailed through wild ostinatos.

———

Once, at the table, my mother asked what I was smiling about. Haejin, she said.

I blinked, Libich vibrating in my head. I, I don't—

She laughed. It's all right, she said. I ate while she peeled a white peach. The skin dropped in a single coil. She picked it up, holding it to the light. Such a rich hue, she said. It flushed pink, backlit; I nodded, then she put it down. I could tell she wished to talk, but I was lost in trills. I pushed a last peach slice in my mouth, and I went back to the piano.

Until then, nothing I played had evoked the orphic singing I knew to be possible. It was an ideal I lacked the skill to bring to life. Each first-place prize marked a point when I'd let the music down. With Libich, I failed less. His étude asked so much of me that, at times, I'd forget I had an I. I should have learned, from this, that playing had to be birthed in a place without ego, in which I didn't exist except as the living conduit, Libich's medium. But then, when I showed the teacher what I could do, he was astonished. I'd achieved more than he'd hoped, he said. He switched the piece in for the next competition, a city-level open. I was driven to the recital hall. The sun fell on my hands as I practiced Libich again, fingers dancing across my legs. Spotlit, I listened to the traffic sing my name. The lax blue of L.A., heat-rippled, veiled the horizon. Like curtains, I thought, poised to rise.

4.

WILL

I first met Phoebe in a house full of strangers, five weeks into the Edwards fall term. I was new to the Noxhurst school, but a sophomore, a late arrival. I'd transferred in from the Bible college I'd had to leave, and I was often on my own. Then, one night, while I was taking a walk alone, I noticed a loud throng of students turning into a gate. It was left propped open; I followed them in. Hip-hop pulsed, rolled. Pale limbs shone. I'd learned that the alcohol table was the one place where I could stand without looking too isolated, and I was idling at my usual station, finishing a third drink, when a girl in a striped dress tripped. She spilled cold liquid down my leg.

She shouted apologies, then a name: Phoebe Lin. Will Kendall, I said, also in a shout. We tried talking, but I kept mishearing what she said. Phoebe started tilting her pelvis from side to side. Life as a juvenile born-again hadn't put me on a lot of dance floors; uncertain, I followed the girl's lead. She swayed left, right, bare shoulders sliding. Others writhed to the frenzied tempo, but Phoebe's hips beat out a slowed-down song. Punch-stained red cups split underfoot, opening into plastic petals. Palms open, she levitated both hands. The room clattered into motion, rising to spin. She dipped, glided along its tilt, and still she moved to the calm rhythm she'd found, dragging the beat until my pulse joined hers.

She kept dancing, so I did, too. By the time she stopped, she looked flushed, out of breath. She lifted black, long hair into a makeshift ponytail. We shouted again, and I watched a drop of sweat trickle from Phoebe's hairline toward the clavicle niche, where it might pool, I thought, to be lapped up. Thick bangs, damp at the tips, parted to expose her forehead. I wanted to kiss that spot, its sudden openness: I leaned down. She pulled close.

Since then, three weeks ago, we talked; we kissed, but that was all. I didn't know what I had the right to ask. I waited, while the rest of Edwards played musical beds. Late at night, if I walked to the bathroom, I crossed paths with still more girls listing tipsily down the hall in oversized, borrowed polo shirts. They flashed smiles, then swerved back into my suitemates' rooms. I returned to mine, but I could still hear the squeals, the high-pitched cries. In no time, a pretty girl might zigzag into my

bed, and if it hadn't happened yet, it was excitingly attainable—
if I said the right words, reached for the right girl—

Instead, on the nights I couldn't sleep, I imagined Phoebe's
sidling hips, the fist-sized breasts. She flailed and squirmed.
With an arched back, rosebud ass soaring up, she starred in solo
fantasies. The fact that I still hadn't slept with Phoebe, or anyone, didn't preclude these scenarios. If anything, it helped. Irri-
tation absolved me of the guilt I might have felt about the uses
to which I put the spectral mouth and breasts. Each time this
ghost Phoebe jumped in my lap, I bit her lips. I licked fingers;
I grabbed fistfuls of made-up skin until, sometimes, when I saw
the girl in the flesh, she looked as implausible as all the Phoebes
I'd dreamed into being.

I pushed through a revolving door into the Colonial: a private
club, college-affiliated. She'd invited me to have a drink. One
last date, I'd resolved. With Phoebe, I kept spending time I
didn't have. I rushed from classes to Michelangelo's, an Italian
restaurant fifteen miles from Noxhurst's town limits—distant
enough, I hoped, that no fellow students would walk in. I took
the bus. I waited tables; I relied on staff meals. I filched apples
from the Edwards dining hall. I received scholarship funding,
but not enough. I told no one.

She was sitting alone at the bar, back facing out. I touched the girl's waist, and she slipped down from the stool. Phoebe's smile, angling up, floated toward me. She asked the bow-tied barkeep, Bix, to bring me a gimlet.

You'll love it, Will, she said. Bix makes, no joke, the world's best gimlets. He puts something extra in. I've asked, but he won't tell me what it is.

If it was my recipe to give, I would, he said.

I believed him. It was obvious he liked Phoebe. She asked how I was, and I said I'd passed a man playing the fiddle while I walked here. I'd paused, to listen. I had no small bills, so I'd put quarters in his upside-down hat. Oh, ho, he said. It's high-rolling time. It's like jingle bells tonight.

He threw out the coins, I said, to Phoebe. I forced a smile, but I hadn't told the story well. I'd tried to help him. Six quarters, which he'd thrown to the ground, like nothing. If I could just tell him as a gag, I'd negate his ridicule. But then, as though she heard the version I intended, Phoebe obliged me, and laughed. She asked what I'd said next. I rattled along. I was pleased; unsettled, too. It was odd, how well she listened. It made me anxious I'd reveal more than I should. When I could, I turned the questions: an old evangelist's trick. In general, people love talking about themselves. If, at times, with Phoebe, I felt a slight resistance, I pushed through.

It's my first time in the Colonial, I said. I asked if she came here often. She explained the club's rituals and traditions, its complicated drinking-cup rules. A ghost-white candle stub guttered between us. I kept asking questions. I liked watching Phoebe talk. She halted, circled the point. Lit up with her own stories, she laughed in big gusts that blew out the candle flame. Bix relit it; before long, she put it out again.

You pass the cup around until it's finished, she said. The last person to drink upends it on his head. He spins it while people sing—

She fell silent, gaze fixed to my left. I turned, but I noticed nothing unusual. Lilies splayed open on the windowsill, wilting stars. A tall man waited at the stoplight.

I thought I saw him again, she said.

Who?

His name's John Leal—do you know him?

I don't think so.

No, it's nothing, she said. I just, I keep thinking I've spotted him, but—

Who is this?

Flustered, she tried to explain. Bix lit the candle, and she thanked him. It took a few tries, but, at last, I gathered she'd gone to a club the other night, downtown. She stepped outside, phone in hand, to call a taxi. Someone else was also there, leaning against the wall. When she hung up, he hailed Phoebe by name. She didn't recognize him, but figured she was to blame. They'd met. She'd forgotten. To be polite, she played along, as if she knew him, but he ignored the act. I'm John Leal, he said.

You're Phoebe. I hoped I'd run into you. I thought of how to set it up, and look, here you are.

Then, he listed small facts about her life. Trivial details, but nothing he should have known. He handed a folded note to Phoebe. I'd love to see you again, he said. It's up to you, though. Call me when you're tired of wasting this life.

When you're tired of—huh, I said.

Isn't it strange? Phoebe said. Oh, also, he had no shoes on. I thought, at first, that friends might be playing a practical joke on me. But it's not much of a joke.

She lifted a glass to Bix. From the level above us, male voices united in song, a capella. I asked if she intended to get in touch with this John Leal. No, but she wished she'd asked how he knew what he did. She'd kept the note, she said, pulling a slip from her wallet. It was plain, lined, ripping along the fold. In block letters, he'd printed his name. John Leal. I suggested she give him a call.

Why?

It's bothering you, I said. If you want, I'll help. I could see him with you.

Just then, a large man popped up behind Phoebe, sliding his hands across her eyes. Guess who, he said. He raised his arms. A full lilac robe spilled out from beneath his peacoat, a priest's white band at his throat. No, don't get up, he said. I've left Liesl outside in the cold, and I told her I wouldn't be a minute but hello, Phoebe, don't you look tip-top. Tell me if you like this outfit. One of Liesl's friends is hosting a themed night: come as you aren't.

So, you're going as the pope, Phoebe said. Or a curtain.

Curtain, he said. *No.* I'm a bishop, and I have a friend with me, a pocket-sized child. This little, pocket-sized protégé . . .

Lifting his coat to the side, he showed us a rag doll in plaid shorts, its mouth attached to his robe, at his crotch. It's a little boy, he said. Phoebe, I want to be introduced.

This is Will Kendall. Will, this is Julian Noh. You've—

Oh, you're Will, he said. He whirled toward me, his robe flaring. Of course, you are. I'm delighted. Phoebe's told me all about you.

Julian, Phoebe said.

Yes.

The doll, she said.

I know, it's brilliant. I mean, he is. He's a brilliant little child, so gifted. Oh, please. It's an homage. I'm paying tribute to the Church, with its, hm, sacerdotal—I think Liesl's waving at me. I'm going. If you want to find us, we'll be at 161 Lowell all night. You, too, Will. Let's be friends.

He thumbed a cross on top of Phoebe's head, and left. So, that's Julian, I said. She'd talked about him: a close friend, the first person she'd met at Edwards. I asked what he'd said about an homage, and she explained he was raised Catholic. But he's since quit the faith, she said.

I had more questions, but singing burst out again. Three additional men, friends of Phoebe, tumbled toward us. They sported loose ties, silk leashes they'd pulled free. She introduced everyone, using full names. They asked if they'd see us at Phil Buxton's tonight. She'd told me she had to go home in a little while: to fit in a bit of studying, for once, she'd said. But they teased Phoebe; they cajoled, like puppies. I smiled at jokes I didn't understand. I'd attended Jubilee, the Bible college in California, until I lost my faith, at which point I'd had to give up a long-held plan to assign my life to God. I then applied to new schools, including Edwards, as distant from California as I could get. Child evangelical that I'd been, I knew as little about pop culture as I did about East Coast shibboleths. Why did Edwards men wear so much pink, and what, exactly, was a—cocksin? No, a coxswain.

But Phoebe, think of Buxton! the three men cried. It's his birthday, no less. While they begged, I kept smiling. She showed a wide slice of throat each time she laughed. Blood surged up the sharp, pale incline of her face. The tips of her ears burned red. I imagined Phoebe sprawled in bed, a thin dress pulled up like a blown magnolia. The halfwit lout on top, his pants down. I thought about what I'd offered Phoebe. I figured it would be a joke, this John Leal riddle. Phoebe's friends loved plotting intricate pranks; they hosted lavish parties, springing naked through college lawns. Oh, fine, I'll go, she said. The silk-tied trio high-fived. But joke or not, I still couldn't tell Phoebe I'd help, then claim I had no time to date, and I felt as relieved about what I'd promised as though I hadn't also been the fool trying to split us apart.

———

I asked Bix if I could settle the tab. Phoebe offered to pay, but I said no, I had it. She waited with me for the bill. You have a lot of friends, I said.

Do I?

Well, even while we've been sitting here, I said. If you tallied up all the people who stopped to say hello.

She glanced around, looking a little absent, as though she'd already started leaving. If anything, I think I know all the alcoholics, she said.

———

But I'm wondering if that can be right, if I met Julian in his lilac bishop's garb when I also first heard about John Leal, or if I've combined multiple Colonial visits, all of them with bow-tied Bix mixing his gimlets, the nights melting like ice slivers into one God-struck evening. I think I'm sure, though, about this sequence. It's possible these are just the details I've saved. It could be grief's narrowed vision: I've noticed what I've lacked.

I am certain that, after my first night at the Colonial, I woke up early the next morning. I had to study for an upcoming exam. Head aching, I was still puzzling through a problem set when I heard the dull roars of a crowd. I didn't want to lose time; I resisted curiosity as long as I could, then I dropped the pen. I unlatched the casement window, pushing it open. Down on the street, crowns of heads bobbed, marching.

No! More! Kills! No! More! Kills!

Who was killing whom? Still in my boxers, naked from the waist up, I leaned across the sill into the cold, trying to make out the words on a sign. Instead, I saw, or I thought I saw, a pink hallucination, a large infant floating against light-blue skies. I blinked, then it was a puppet, held up with barbershop-striped poles. It lolled on its back, the fat strung limbs shining.

In the news, I would read that the baby was ten feet tall, assembled from cloth and foam by protest organizers, and that the crowd was rallying against an abortion clinic that had opened in downtown Noxhurst; for now, as I strained, I could make out overtly Christian placards. Depictions of the cross, mentions of God. I watched the protest pass, sick with longing. Such a lot of people who still believed they were picked to be God's children. The unreal baby jiggled its fists, as in the divine visions I once hoped to have, the marvels I'd thought possible. The nephilim at hand, radiant galaxies pirouetting at God's command. Faith-lifted mountains. Miracles. Healings. I turned Christian in junior high, the first time my mother fell ill. It's a crack across the brain, she explained. It let sadness in. Pills helped, like a patch, but the usual medicine had stopped working. Lying in bed, she gazed at the ceiling fan. She didn't wash. Each morning, I left a glass of milk on the bedside table. She ignored it, and the milk curdled. My father came home late, stumbling. He broke lamps; he slept in the living room.

So, I prayed. I was devoted. A kid evangelist, and a pain in the ass. I traipsed through town in ironed khakis, pocket Bible in hand, testifying. I made it a personal mission to save my parents, as well: I didn't want paradise unless I could bring them along. Though my father laughed at my improvised lectures, my mother let me talk. In bed, pallid, she listened. I proselytized until the June afternoon, five months into my campaign, when I stood witness at her baptism. She waded into the lake in a yellow poplin dress, and I shook with pride. The pastor put his hands on her shoulders. She plunged in, submerged so long I panicked, thinking she'd drown, but then he let go. She came up flailing, smiling to break her mouth. The lake healed itself around her hips. In a dress like the sun, she splashed out. She picked me up, spattering lake silt. I touched my mother's head, the hair wet, sanctified. I, I, I—I thought I'd saved her life.

———

Close to noon, as I left my suite, Phoebe called to tell me she'd talked to John Leal. He'd invited us both to dinner, Monday at

8:00. Litton Street. Did I have plans then? I didn't. Would I still be willing to go, in that case? I would, I said. I asked if she'd enjoyed the night. She had. It had gone late. The birthday boy had rented lions.

Lions?

Well, they were caged, she explained.

Phoebe's words lagged, catching in her throat. I asked if she'd just gotten up. Oh, she said, *up* would be a lie. I'm still in bed.

I said I was going to Wyeth Hall for lunch. Did she want to meet me there? Yes, she said. She'd leave in ten minutes. I walked through the quadrangle. It was quiet here, the lawn isolated from the town's noise. I'd first come upon Edwards after days of bus travel from California to upstate New York. I planned to walk the final mile to my hall, but when I left the Noxhurst station and saw the line of taxis, clean with sunlight, I lost all resolve. Minutes later, I paid for the ride. I pulled both suitcases to the curb—

Then, I looked up. I forgot the wasted dollars. The tall, pronged gates stood wide. I rolled my bags through the entryway, a tunnel cored out of a thick wall, and the darkness opened into light. I was in the main quadrangle. Spires and belfries spun up from stone citadels. Frisbees soared. Bronze statues gazed forward, frozen in heroes' poses. Sunlit paths crossed the green, lines in a giant palm, holding students who lazed on the grass. It was a lost garden, but I'd been allowed in. I still hadn't known, though I soon would, how little I'd belong.

I approached the dining hall. I'd been up since six, while she was in bed, idling. Lions in a cage. Had she petted them, and did she wake to find the tawny fur glinting on her skin? She might have rubbed the fur around as she slept. The coarse hairs strewn in Phoebe's sheets, bijou rays of gold. But my step felt light. If I could be anyone, I'd ask to be the Will rushing to see more, again, of Phoebe. In the distance, an advertisement painted on the side of a brick building showed a young girl, lips pursed as if to send a wish. The suck and howl of a siren pierced the cold, and the fall wind smelled of reasons to live.

5.

JOHN LEAL

Three months into his captivity, John Leal was shoved in the back of a truck, driven from the gulag to the frozen riverbank, and told to cross to China. He hesitated; a guard raised his gun, hit him with its butt. Bleeding from his temple, John Leal started walking. It was early March. Thin lines fissured the river's ice. Each spring, the thawed waters were said to clog with all those shot while trying to escape, the bodies preserved, like fish, where they'd been killed.

Behind him, a guard laughed. If they didn't shoot him, they'd watch him plunge through ice, and drown. He tried the next step. Spindrift lifted, fell. Inhale. Exhale. His nerves stretched, a net to span the width of ice dividing him from the rest of his life. Filaments glittered, straining with his weight. China stood prismatic on the opposite side. He let out a long breath. His soul was blowing loose, but he inhaled. He pulled it back in. There was no being afraid. He walked on water with each step. The ice cracked; he held still. Try to live. Take a step again.

6.

PHOEBE

In Phoebe's next confession to Jejah, she might have said: If you love to win, as I did, it's not enough to do well. Others also have to fail. In the past, I'd collected trophies, boxes full, but not like this. With Libich, I swept the top prizes. I left judges in tears. Rival pianists knew who I was, and I had the blood taste of public triumph on my lips. Each time, I wanted more, again. I thought I'd willed it into being, at last, the life I expected. I'd prove what I could do.

Then, six months after I first played Libich for him, the teacher gave me a gift recording, a Libich revival. It was a celebrated album, hard to find. I'd read about this 1951 concert, tales of an ecstatic audience, mass fainting. Now, I hustled to find a shop that sold record players. The fifth étude was the last track, but I forced myself to wait. I played the album in full. The last notes were still fading when I tipped the machine off the side table. It crashed down. The record slid until it hit the wall. I picked it up, and I bent it. The plastic cracked, but I was too late. I'd listened to it. I couldn't pretend I hadn't.

That night, I told my mother I had no option but to quit the piano. I won't be delusional, I said. I didn't have the talent. It wasn't enough to be good. I could see no point in devoting this life to music if I wouldn't add to what leading pianists, the ones I idolized, had achieved. I shouldn't waste time, trying.

I had more to explain, but she smiled as though I were a child, ludicrous. I'd made no sense; I should be indulged. I'm serious, I said, and she laughed.

Of course, you're not, she said. I had to realize what she had lived through. She'd just finished college in Seoul, at the top of the class, when she allowed herself to be trapped. First, she said yes to a proposal. She followed the tradition of moving into a husband's parents' house. His relatives bullied the young bride. On dates, he'd been pliant, docile; in this alien house, she was criticized all day long. It was like being a servant, but with less privilege. Maids get paid. By the time she gave birth, she'd had enough. She left with the child. In months, he trailed them to L.A. He pled, full of apologies, but she'd found a job. It paid so well, they'd given up needing him. She toiled, piled cash. It was all for infant Haejin, a girl who'd get the outsize life she'd been denied.

But I've heard this, I said. No, she said. I hadn't, not if I believed I could quit. Since I wished to be a pianist, I should make it happen. What I wanted, I'd have. I was the one who'd requested a piano. It had been my idea. I had a gift, she said. It was also an obligation. I'd be lost without the music.

––––––

I pulled all the applications to conservatories; accepted at Edwards, I said I would go. But the school also has a piano program, she said. It's why you applied in the first place. Haejin, they'll let you in. We hadn't been in the habit of arguing, but now we couldn't stop. The fight lasted until April, the night of a cello recital. Though I hadn't listened to music since Libich, we'd had the tickets since the previous fall. It wasn't the piano. I'll be fine, I thought, but then string music filled the hall. I'd have given anything to be able to perform as well as I'd hoped I could. It was true, as she said, that I'd started playing the music on my own. I was so small, at first, that I had to sit on a trunk balanced on top of the piano bench. It lifted me up. Disembodied in the piano's polished depths, I hurled back and forth like its possessing spirit, shown large, powerful. I'd loved the piano. I still did. It was too bad. I wiped my face; she noticed. She held out a tissue, but I ignored it. I couldn't admit I'd cried.

The cello recital ended. In the parking lot, I insisted I'd

drive. I had a license, but she didn't often let me behind the wheel; this time, she gave in. Maybe she pitied me. She'd tired of fighting. I didn't ask, and it was the last time we talked. In silence, I drove. I got us a mile from home before I started crying again. Half-blind, I rolled into the opposing lane.

7.

WILL

She picked me up to drive to John Leal's house. Paired taillights
swept ahead of us, the red lamps slewing here, there. Turning off
the road, she hurtled uphill, and stopped. Phoebe and I walked
up the flagstone path to a white, tall house. She held my hand,
swinging it, the way children do. Piled leaves blew about, alive
again. She touched the bell button. I lifted Phoebe's hand; I
kissed bitten nails that shine, in hindsight, like quartz, spoils
I pulled down from the moon.

———

The door flung open. Strangers appeared, drawing us into the
heat, the light. The rich perfume of cooked flesh filled the front

hall. Saliva flooded my mouth. They asked if we'd mind removing our shoes. Light-headed, I used the excuse to crouch. I took in a breath as I unknotted the tight laces. I hadn't eaten since morning, when I had a stolen Gala apple. With the bus behind schedule, I'd arrived at Michelangelo's too late for the staff lunch.

Phoebe and I were led down a hall, into the living room. Flat blue cushions had been placed in a half-circle in front of the lit fireplace. There was no furniture. Invited to sit, I followed Phoebe's lead: I took a cushion, the one closest to hers. It slipped as I sat, the glossed fabric smooth.

Is John Leal here? Phoebe asked. I'd love to tell him hello.

He's in the kitchen, they said. He'll join us in a minute. Before long, the conversation split in two. Phoebe chatted with a girl whose name I hadn't caught, then with a person called Ian. He left the room, coming back with full porcelain teacups. Mulled wine, he said. Meanwhile, I jolted through pleasantries with Philip Hecht, also an Edwards student. I wondered when they'd reveal the punchline behind this evening. When, not if, I still thought. Philip asked where I was from; the girl, Jo, smiled. I started reciting lies I'd been telling since the first day in Noxhurst, the half-truths ballooning until, in moments, I turned into a different Will again, floating above the usual Kendall problems. I cut the strings. I had the balloonatic's glee. Timelines cracked, shifted; my father pulled his emptied seat to the table. My mother's little rental house sailed south from dull, meth-addled Carmenita to the hills of Los Angeles, expanding mid-flight into an open villa with the kind of misshapen pool no one but the rich would have. It lit up at night. I swam in its blue fire.

While I talked, the mulled wine's spiced heat coiled into me, melting caution, as on that first hot fall afternoon when I climbed three flights up Latham Hall, dragging bags. I'd found my suite-mates in the living room, five men in polo shirts: about to go eat, they said, inviting me along. We shook hands. They were all sophomores, like me, but they'd been friends as freshmen. Jovial, polite, offering help with the luggage, they asked about my trip to Edwards: if I'd flown, or driven.

I took the bus, I said. Well, multiple buses—from California—

For a long instant, they looked alike, faces tight with surprise. By the time they rallied, I'd revised how I should be. My mother's Pasadena family, rich but dissolute, had misspent the last of its fortune when she was still old enough to recall the luminous idyll she'd lost, and I could use the hacienda memories. Palm trees rising tall, June-night operas at the Hollywood Bowl. I drew on this inherited longing. I filled in peripheral details that helped me settle into who I was: that pool, for instance, the occasional fat plop as fruit from sunlit citrus trees ripens, drowns. In this life of blue honey, I don't think of the waste. I lap; I crawl. Navel oranges shine from the tiles like medallions. A hired man whistles, fishing out the rot. No one lacks food, or falls ill.

I tried to ask questions of Philip, as well. But he acted pre-occupied, glancing past my head. The next time his eyes flicked up, I turned, too—I saw the figure at the doorsill, a clean white apron knotted around his waist. I saw him float; I looked again, and it was the filth, a half-inch of skin stained black at his soles, the heels split, flaking. Noticing I'd seen him, he nodded. He walked toward us, holding wine-glass bouquets in his fingers. He wasn't tall, but his shoulder muscles strained against a plain white shirt. His wrist bulged where he'd tied a red string, letting it dig in. With his hair brushed to stand upright, a high plume, I had the sense of a surfeit of energy, not quite contained, like a child's color-book illustration escaping its lines. He turned to me.

It's Will, right? he said, quietly. He set the glasses down, then he took my hand in both of his. I'm John Leal, he said. I'm late. I apologize. I had to supervise the rib eyes. Not such a good choice while having guests, or so I'm learning. You're the first people we've had eat with us in a long time. I'm so glad you're here. We all are. Let's go in.

⸻

In the dining room, we sat at a table set low to the ground, with more silk cushions for seats. A blond girl holding a tray came and left. I wondered what kind of people hired help for a six-top meal. She poured from a bottle of Malbec, the ruby pool looping into my glass. I didn't touch it, though. I was already dizzied with what little I'd tried of the mulled wine.

I'll emphasize this lack of alcohol because, teetotal as I soon felt, I should be able to retrieve more of what followed. Instead, for the most part, it's lost. I have the outline, bits of conversation. Fitful images. Wide swaths of it, though, have blurred as in old film. Is that the problem? I've reviewed this initial feast with them so often I've smudged it with my fingerprints. Pink meat bled when I cut it open, the charred bits crunching like minute bones. A torn roll steamed; butter liquefied. Oil dripped, gilding white porcelain. The waitress's thin wrist shook as she removed a plate. I said thanks, and she flinched. Inexperience, I assumed. Teeth flashed, smiling. Of all people, I should have recognized this warmth for what it was: a bag of tricks. The fellowship, a little food. The hocus-pocus bribe of hot bread, lavish, like God: take, eat. This is my body, which is broken for you. Open curtains exposed a line of sash windows. In the depths of the glass, silhouettes, our best selves, bent and moved. I felt seen for what I wanted to be. I relaxed, and I had more food.

Citron tarts finished, we returned to the living room. In the uncertain firelight, the cushions shone lazulite blue. Phoebe and

John Leal sat off to one side, apart from the rest of us. Each time I looked at them, he was still talking. She stared down, into her lap. Her hair draped, its fall pushing forward a ribbon head-band.

—too loyal to this suffering, you forget that others are also in pain, he said, barely audible.

I'm not, she said, glancing up at him. I don't think I am.

No. I don't think you are.

The waitress walked around offering tea, mulled wine. Tea, please, I said. Fine hair hung loose as she tipped the pot, biting her lip. Phoebe had a handbag at her side, partially zipped, and while they talked, I watched John Leal pick it up, open it, and put his hand inside. He rifled through it, still talking. I'd held that bag for Phoebe; I knew the feel of its plush, living calfskin. I thought of my mother's handbag, the box-shaped satchel so pri-vate I'd seen its full contents just once in my life, while she was being held in the hospital. I had to sign for the possessions, ini-tialing each item. Hand-sanitizing gel. Labeled pills. Fish oil, aspirin. Lipstick. Jojoba lotion. Rape whistle. I hadn't admitted to what I couldn't help seeing: she'd have hated the intrusion, but Phoebe, unperturbed, kept gazing at his face. He dipped his fingers into the bag's opal slit. The bright satin lining showed. I'd have liked to stop him, but she let it happen. The bag might as well have been his.

Ill at ease, I left to find a bathroom. I returned to find everyone standing while Philip rolled in an upright piano. He pushed it against the wall, lid open. Ian carried in a cushioned bench, and Phoebe walked toward the instrument. I asked Jo what was going on. She explained that Ian usually played the piano, but he'd injured his thumb. Phoebe had agreed to fill in.

She——, I said, but I stopped. Phoebe sat at the bench. She twisted a knob, adjusting its height. Not long ago, we'd been walking past the grand piano in Wyeth Hall. It gleamed with disuse, and I said I'd never seen anyone touch it. Such a waste, I said. It's not a good piano, though, she said. I asked if she played. Oh, she said. No.

The first notes tolled. Phoebe's hands moved, pressing out slow chords, but she sat up, torso rigid, as if she had nothing to do with the music. Fingers rippled, gaining speed. The solo line of Phoebe's right hand jumped high. She came to life. Holding the note, she flexed toward the piano. She turned her head, listening. It echoed, and I could imagine the walls of this house falling down, Noxhurst flattened, the rest of the world blown to nothing until it was just Phoebe, still holding this single, light note. She swept a hand down across the keys, and she kept playing.

———

When the front door clicked shut behind us, Phoebe asked if I minded driving. I'm full of wine, she said, loud, through high wind. She pulled hair strands out of her mouth. Did you drink as much as I did? No, of course you didn't. You exercised self-control. I used to know how to do such a thing, but I've lost the trick. I could call a taxi.

I'll drive, I said. Inside the car, its abrupt hush, I could still feel the last piano notes thrum, radiant: a faint light, haloing the quiet. I switched on the ignition. I hadn't studied an instrument. For years, though, while eluding the devil's influence, I'd listened to classical music. I owned piano recordings I loved. Lupu, for instance. Gould. Uchida. Wasn't it Liszt, what she'd played? I was trying to establish bona fides. Once, while hiking with my parents, I'd watched a starling flock in motion, the confusion of birds mobbing about like nets full of fish until they'd lifted, all at once, shape-shifting into a braided coil that flung, agile, whip-tight, into the horizon. Pests, my father said—practical, as usual. But I'd thought it an astonishing sight, God's design made visible, and that was what Phoebe's playing felt like: the flight of notes rising into shape, a large purpose made plain. You should be onstage, I said. If I had a gift like that, I'd—

You'd live for it, she said. You, Will Kendall, would be a celebrated pianist, a high priest of music.

I don't know why you're laughing.

No, it's, I tried. I wanted to be a pianist. I'm not sure that's what it is, a gift. By the time I quit, I realized I'd rather have no talent than just enough to know how much I lacked. I played tonight because he insisted. That's all. He was telling me about his time in the gulag, and I—

"He" being John, I started saying, my voice overlapping hers.

I couldn't turn him down—

The gulag?

Oh, she said.

He was in a gulag.

Oh, Will.

In the spring, two years ago—

(so Phoebe explained, turned toward me, a hand hot on my thigh as I sped through emptied Noxhurst streets, past the stoplights staining the night)

—John Leal had gone to live in Yanji, a Chinese city next to North Korea. He worked with an activist group, with Americans who helped North Koreans in hiding get out of China, into Seoul. It was a long, roundabout trip that required walking through the Laotian jungle, so hazardous they relied on opium mules as guides. Then, one night, he was seized by North Korean spies who took him across the border, throwing him into a gulag. He still couldn't talk much about what he witnessed. Lives thrown out like trash, he said. A five-year-old child hanged for stealing a little rice. Gang rapes. Everyone was starving. Deprived of rations, a man had eaten the shit-soiled rags used to wipe latrines. One corpse was found stashed in ice, his missing parts marked with human teeth. He watched prison guards kicking a pregnant girl in the stomach. She curled around the swollen belly, trying to protect it. They left the girl bleeding on the ground.

People turned aside, afraid. John Leal, too. But then, he noticed an old man helping the girl up, and he was ashamed. In secret, John Leal nursed the girl, Mina. He applied the primitive first-aid training he'd learned from his activist group. She had lived in hiding in China until hostile neighbors alerted the police. The minute she was told she'd be sent back, she'd known what would happen: since foreign blood was believed to be a pollution, the regime aborted all babies conceived abroad. She cried for the child she'd lose. He did his best, but he couldn't stop the bleeding. That night, Mina died, along with the unborn child.

Five months after his abduction, he was driven with no explanation to the Chinese border, beaten, and told to cross the frozen river back into Yanji. He did: he survived, but he was down thirty pounds, his left arm broken. In this shape, he couldn't help his group, so he returned to the States. The girl he failed to save, Mina, traveled with him. Each night, when he tried to sleep, she materialized next to his bed. He asked what she wished him to do, but she didn't respond. Lips tight, she watched him. It took several nights to notice she wasn't wearing shoes. In life, she'd owned sandals that he'd given to a shoeless inmate when Mina died. He asked if this was what she wanted, shoes. She ignored the question.

The next morning, on an impulse, he went outside shoeless. He stood on cold asphalt, holding up a sign to raise cash for Yanji activists. From that night on, Mina's spirit left him alone. He kept fundraising in bare feet. In time, he learned to focus his canvassing efforts on big, Korean American churches. First along the East Coast, and then the West. He was Korean, himself; half-Korean, that is.

Phoebe's father helped his campaign: he invited John Leal up to the pulpit with him. It was how John Leal had known about Phoebe. He'd mentioned having attended Edwards to Reverend Lin, who then talked about his own child, also Noxhurst-bound. Oh, her father's church—she thought she'd talked about it. Oh. Well, he'd founded a church in L.A. She wasn't the least bit religious, no. Her parents had split up when she was little.

So, the Yanji group—it had lost a second activist, then a third. Both abducted, perhaps killed. The group then disbanded. With no fundraising left to do, John Leal had returned to Noxhurst to work at a nonprofit, a legal-aid organization advising recent immigrants. It was useful work, he said, but less satisfying. He wanted to help people firsthand. Instead, he filled in official forms. He solicited grants. The people we'd met at his

house thought as he did, hoping to shape their lives around public service. Now, he was looking around, waiting to find what
he'd do next.

———

By the time Phoebe finished telling me this, we were back on
campus, cutting across the quadrangle lawn. I didn't know how
I should respond. Fall leaves crunched, splintered with each
step. We passed a bulletin board, its slats pulped with old
notices. I knew about lying; I recognized its signs. In the months
to come, I'd listen to still more versions of John Leal's gulag
tale, his shifting harlequin cast. The penitent assassin. The
ex-trapezist, who escaped. The spy, the kingpin. He even invented a hanged child to fill out this troupe plucked from a
fortune-teller's pack of obvious lies, and I can't recall which version I heard first. What Phoebe said gets spliced with his future
inventions. I strain to pull them apart. I fail. John Leal intrudes
even here, as I walk with Phoebe along the wet, short grass.

She asked what I was thinking, but I couldn't find a good
rebuttal. I felt a nervous smile sliding up my face, the kind I can't
help using with people who believe.

That's incredible, I said.

Isn't it?

So, John Leal found you because, he hoped to—

Well, when I enrolled here, my father asked him to look out

for me. I asked why he made such a riddle out of it, and he said, If the first thing I told you was that I'm your father's friend, would you still have wanted to talk to me?

A small crowd passed, laughing. Someone called hello to Phoebe; she blew him a kiss. You're not close with him? I asked.

He lived in L.A., too, thirty minutes from us, but I didn't see much of him. It was complicated, the divorce. I wasn't raised to believe as he does. I didn't go to church at all, and his church is his life. It bothered him that I'm not Christian. I'm sure it still does.

I hesitated. She hadn't mentioned a religious upbringing; I knew I'd alluded to mine. I'd joked about it, I was sure. When *I* was a Christian, I said, at times, playing my life's pivotal loss as a joke. Now, I told Phoebe that I'd attended a Bible college before Edwards. Up until I stopped believing in God, I said. I thought I was chosen by Christ. Hand-picked to preach His word. Don't laugh, but I used to peddle salvation outside of town bars, hoping to catch drunks when they'd be extra sentimental. It worked, too. I was good at it. In the back of my Bible, I listed all the souls I saved.

I'm not laughing, she said.

I'd kept my tone light, but I felt Phoebe's increased attention, like heat. I looked at the ground. I haven't talked to anyone here about it, I said.

Do you mind if I ask what made you stop believing?

It was nothing special, I said. The usual host of reasons.

Like what?

Oh, the existence of multiple religions, children starving. The problem of evil—it's how people talk about going bankrupt, right? It's gradual, then it happens all at once.

Trampling leaves, we walked toward Platt Hall. It must have been so hard, though, she said, expanding. She intended to sympathize, I could tell, and it was true: I'd tried not to leave the faith. I'd had such purpose, living in single-minded pursuit of the God I loved, until the afternoon I knelt in my bedroom, asking one last time for a sign. White gauze curtains rippled. I waited, but I heard nothing else. Muscles stiff, I got up. I should, I think, have told Phoebe how cut open I felt since then, with a God-shaped hole I didn't know how to fill. If I was sick of Christ, it was because I hadn't been able to stop loving Him, this made-up ghost I still grieved as though He'd been real. For a while, train tracks had pulled. So had guns, pills, but already I wished I hadn't brought this up. I didn't want Phoebe pitying me. To change the subject, I asked about the hired help, the nervous blond girl.

Tess, Phoebe said. No, she wasn't hired. She lives with them. They all rotate serving meals. I had more questions, but the door to Phoebe's hall slammed open. Girls in high heels clattered out; she caught the knob before it could swing closed. She asked if I wanted to come in. I walked into the stone stairwell. Steps echoing, we climbed. We passed through the suite living room, into Phoebe's single. Silence rushed between us. The tip of Phoebe's tongue brightened her lips. It was the first time she'd invited me in.

I have gin, she said.

Do you want a drink?

If you will.

I can, I said. Sure.

She stepped down from her heels. While she cracked out ice cubes, I shook off my oxfords. I wandered the small room. There wasn't much to see: she'd left the walls blank. A tall pile of textbooks lay unopened, the plastic wrap shining. She passed me a fizzing glass with a lime slice split across its rim, then tapped laptop keys. A bass hiss drifted from the speakers. It's a Spanish band, she said. Did I like it? I said I did, and she began swaying to the song's loose beat. Bare shoulders rolled. She snapped her fingers overhead, imitating castanets.

I danced with her for the length of the song, and then she unfastened my pants. She stripped me down to my boxers. I haven't done this before, I thought of saying; I didn't. It wasn't until I was naked that she let me pull off her shirt, its striped, delicate fabric bunching in my palms. I unzipped Phoebe's skirt. I'd fantasized about this for weeks, in detail. Even as I slid a nail up the ridged line of the real Phoebe's spine, those previous versions, ghostly but alive, crowded around us. They flexed thin backs, exhaling phantom sighs while I tried to focus on this girl, Phoebe, with these specific ribs. Fingers with this exact tang of lime juice. We fell in bed. I put Phoebe's thumb in my mouth; I lapped at taut nipples. She lowered a breast to brush my lips, then raised it again, playful. But when I tried to roll on top, she resisted.

What's wrong? I asked.

Let's stay like this, she said. She straddled me, then shifted onto hands and knees. She looked back, shoulders arched, and instructed me to keep going. Small hipbones jutted out like half-formed handles; I reached for them. She rocked back and forth, but I still couldn't tell if she was having a good time. I heard a branch scratch the windowpane, insistent. The sound emphasized Phoebe's silence. It was too soon to stop. I tried to think. The other night, while it rained, a gingko had fallen. In the morning, a passerby noticed a white gleam in its root ball. It turned out to be a skull. The Edwards quadrangle had been built on top of an old burial site. Beneath the lawn, the earth would be latticed with bones. I bent low, kissing the knotted spine. I wanted to slow down. Phoebe thrust back against my thighs. It was too fast, too—she tensed at the waist. Letting go, I collapsed.

8.

JOHN LEAL

The fall he returned to Noxhurst, John Leal established a habit of paying morning visits to the graves on Hilcox Street. The churchyard gates opened at dawn. He went in to keep his vigil. Tall lindens stood bare, stripped by the cold, but still they raised their limbs in hallelujah. He walked about; he examined memorial inscriptions, the etched, once-loved names fading. Frost burned his feet. Winter softened into spring, and mossed obelisks pointed on high. In the estival heat, he set his back against the cold stone of a tomb. He plucked a honeysuckle stalk sprouting from what had once been men; he sipped its bit of juice. In time, lying in the dirt, he, too, might nourish future pilgrims. If he had one petition for himself, it was this: that he be made useful.

But he was learning to be patient. His plan stood intelligible to him, lucid as a vision. If asked, before the gulag, how a revelation might look, a heraldic blaze of light would have come to mind, the flap and gust of gale-force wind. His own dazzled, indisputable rip in the fabric of the usual. Instead, he had this: a plan. His chance. He lifted his face. Through linden branches, blue lozenges flashed like prizes he could reach up to have. His personal ambitions, though, no longer signified. He was thinking of mankind. In the months to come, when Phoebe asked about his first revelation, he'd explain it had arrived with a shock of recognition—yes, he'd thought. This was it. He'd been waiting. In fact, he said, to Phoebe, I felt like this when I first heard of you.

9.

PHOEBE

I collided into a truck, she'd have said. I'm trying to imagine it: Phoebe, sitting with the group again, legs pulled in. Posture like a ball, a full-bodied fist. The others in a circle, staring while she exposes her life.

The truck driver broke his leg, Phoebe said. I wasn't hurt. My mother absorbed all the impact. She bled to death before she could be taken to the hospital. I was still in high school, underage, so I had to go live in my father's house.

I hadn't spent much time with him, growing up. My mother's plan, once she left Seoul, was to raise me alone. But then, he followed us to the States, pleading to live with us again. She didn't let him, at first. When she did relent, it was because she thought I'd benefit from having both parents around. Often, they fought;

he turned violent, at times. I sat at the top of the stairs, one night, while they shouted. He punched her, and she fell. She didn't get up, so I ran down. I thought she'd died. She wasn't moving. I wanted to call for help, but he took a glass of water from the dinner table. He splashed it on her face until she woke up. Still, she kept trying. I was five before she asked me if I'd be all right if she left him again. If we left, she said. You and I. I said yes, let's go. I picked sides at once.

He stayed civil, though, when I had to move in with him. Polite, like a distant relative. He didn't even ask if I wanted to come to his church. He might have believed I'd refuse. I noticed him crying, in the kitchen: I pretended I hadn't. If he was grieving, I didn't think he had the right.

I finished the last month of high school. Then, as soon as possible, I left. I came to Noxhurst. In Littell, during the college president's opening talk, I walked out. I crossed the silent campus while everyone else sat in chapel pews, listening to the president tell them how glad they should feel. This school, he'd said. He called it one of the nation's pinnacles of learning. Such luck. Privilege. The obligation to give back. In front of Latham gate, a fellow truant held a bluish flame up to the key-card light. The gate didn't open; the flame went out. He flicked his flame on again. I asked what he was doing.

It's broken, he said. This gate. It's busted. Won't open.

I could give it a try, I said.

He paused, but then he stepped back. His broad face was

pink, sullen. The tall bulk of him listed toward the stone arch. I swiped my card, and the gate rang open. I tried not to laugh. He said I was his hero. You'll have to let me give you a drink, he insisted, until I followed him to his suite. He told me his name, Julian. Julian Noh. I gave him mine. He asked if I was also Korean, lifting his hand for a high five. I could tell, he said. Tilting into his futon, he slid on his back, sighed, then closed his eyes. I tiptoed as I left. In the morning, I had a waist-high bouquet, white gladioli, propped against the doorsill. It included a long note from Julian, apologizing. He requested that I come to his suite to join him in, as he put it, a wine-tasting shindig. I did, and then I went with him to more parties, not getting back to my place until dawn. We split a late lunch that afternoon.

Phoebe, he said. Last night, you met a Mitch. Blond, kind of thin, this high. Tell me if you liked him. I do, I think.

I asked Julian questions. He tried to reciprocate, asking about life before Edwards. No, I said. First, I have to know everything about you. I want all your secrets, Julian. Let's start at the beginning. Big or small, what's the first lie you told? I watched him smile, each wide tooth showing. It was like a picket fence swinging open: his smile invited me inside.

Since I had Julian as a guide, I started meeting the Edwards students admitted into this pinnacle of learning with the single purpose, from what I could see, of having fun. To flaunt the privilege. In thrift-store ballgowns, they splashed through off-limits fountains. Champagne foamed like gold dissolving.

Open up, like a good girl, Julian said, a white pill glinting in his palm. I tipped back my head. The pills split time. I flopped on the wet lawn to cool down. Light spilled from open doors. Drunks lurched, spun. Silhouettes flared into detail, then fizzled out again. I woke late, head muddled. Lunch lasted hours. I piled up invitations. I switched roles with Julian, taking him places. He followed along, gleeful. Don't forget, though, he said. I've called dibs on you. Hands off, I tell them. She's all mine.

Oh, but I wasn't. Before Will, I had, for instance, the squash recruit who liked sucking toes. The poet who kept a ball pit in his suite's living room. Girl bait, he said. Phil, who pissed in the hall closet because, late at night, he believed it to be a bathroom stall, and Tim, who lined his room with emptied wine bottles, like trophies. But no, I don't mean to be glib. I got in the habit, with friends, Julian, of turning one-night flings into stories. The truth is, I wince if I think of that first month at Edwards. I recall it in pieces: ill-lit body parts, lip balm–glossed penises. Pinched nipples. Elbows and bad aim. They'd wheeze, then mild pain. Is that all right? they'd ask. I lied, to be kind.

I drank a lot. In bars, I left full drinks unattended. Then, I gulped them down. If I failed to be careful, she might notice. She'd have to come back. One night, I put on the shortest dress I owned, and then I sat on a low wall on the edge of campus, legs dangling. Red lights spotted the intersection. I watched the crowd pass, thinking, Pick me up, until someone did. He didn't have protection. It's fine, I said. Go ahead.

Downtown, in a split-level dive called Levi's, I fell into conversation with Greg, a local, a high-school dropout in his thirties. I'd first met him because he sold Julian drugs. I went home with Greg, then I let him tie me to his bed. He fucked me through a hole he razored open in my tights. I shared a bottle of gin with him; I felt light-headed, ill, until I woke in a hospital bed.

I was brought in throwing up, a nurse explained. No, I'd come in an ambulance. I had a little too much alcohol, but I'd be all right. The hospital had given me fluids. Hush, doll, she said. You'll be fine.

It was late, almost morning. I left the bed when a man behind the partition began yelling. I was still in the previous night's clothes, though with ankle-length hospital socks covering my feet. Torn tights chafed my crotch. I walked the half-mile home, the sidewalk cold through thin fabric. Mica specks, like felled stars, prickled the stone. But most of it was filth. I avoided broken glass, ripped foil bags. Slicks of fresh dog shit. I picked each step through trash. The sun was rising. I hadn't been allowed outside, when I was a child, without putting on sun lotion. My mother's light, cool hands patted protective liquid on my face. She fastened a wide-brim hat beneath my chin, tying the ribbons in a firm knot, loops aligned. Such pains she'd taken, for the little I'd since become.

10.

WILL

I stayed the night with Phoebe. In the morning, I watched as she slept, netted in white sheets. Nostrils flared with each long inhale. Pearl studs glinted at slim earlobes. Minute, fish-scale veins patterned Phoebe's eyelids in faint blue. The birthmark speckling a left clavicle, slight indents at both temples—from the start, I wanted Phoebe memorized. In the old-gold light of morning, I had the idea she might have been a wild sea-creature who'd washed onshore, luck's gift, legs tucked like a mermaid's tail. I learned to swim before I could walk, she'd said. But I was so involved with the piano, I went three years without using my own pool. It was still early, not quite six. I waited as long as I could; at last, I tried shaking Phoebe awake, but she rolled toward the wall.

I left Platt Hall as a drunk slouched past, the label on his bottle dissolving. I wished he'd solicit cash; in the mood I was in, spilling with goodwill, I'd have relished giving him something. If I'd been riding the bus, I'd have looked around to find a person who could use my seat. Instead, I thought to check my phone, and I saw I'd missed a call. I listened to the message my mother had left: the station-wagon engine had died. In the shop, she'd learned that fixing it would cost hundreds of dollars. While she could enlist a church friend to provide rides to and from work, they lived on opposite sides of town. She needed the engine fixed as soon as possible.

When I knew she'd be up, I called. I don't have the money, not yet, but I'll figure it out, I promised.

What I'd do without you, I don't know, honey, she said. She laughed a little, rueful. The exhale rustled the line, and she almost sounded like her old self again. The mother I'd had used to bring kitchen-table bouquets from the garden: buttercups, dahlia. Goldenrod in armfuls, the paint-daub petals trailing, flickering, like tattered flags. Nose dusted with pollen, she sang Donizetti arias in phonetic Italian. When I was an infant, she waltzed me to bel canto until I slept. She'd been ill a long time; still, it wasn't until last March, in my father's absence, that she first had to be hospitalized. I returned home from a spring-break mission to Beijing, a trip I'd had planned for months, to find she'd moved into the living room, stationed on an airbed to avoid what she'd shared with him. He'd fled to Florida to live with a girlfriend we hadn't known existed. I learned this from the note he left; my mother had stopped talking. The cut flowers had wilted. I changed the vases. When she did, at last, get up, she sat gazing into a compact. Once, as I watched, she brushed lipstick on the reflection.

But when I was hired at Michelangelo's, Paul, who owned the place, had indicated I might attain a future promotion. He could use a college kid like me to help snap the whip, like an assistant-managing type, he said. Since then, he hadn't brought it up. I thought of what I'd spent these past couple of months on clothes. Oxford shirts, marlin-printed shorts. The white-soled boat shoes, out of season until spring. Ribbon belts. In thrift stores, online, in the attempt to look like what I claimed to be, I scavenged polo shirts in pink, azure, and apple green, the bizarrely colorful regalia of the ruling class. I wore the polos layered; I ridged collars upright, like gills. Meanwhile, my mother bagged groceries in Carmenita. I deposited much of what I made in tips into my mother's account, helping with basic necessities: rent, medical bills, but each week I still had a little extra, which, if I'd saved, I could have given at once, instead of asking that she wait.

Fifteen minutes before the gates opened at Michelangelo's, I found Paul. I asked if he'd thought about the promotion he'd said was possible. He stood at the reservations pulpit, writing in his tight script on the back of a menu. Sure, I've thought about it, he said, not looking up. His gold pen scratched out a line.

Is anything decided? I asked.

The pen scraped. His belt-halved gut bulged out, grazing the zinc edge, like an animal about to lunge. It fit his look of menace: if provoked, his flesh might achieve its escape. I glanced past him, trying not to stare. In a torn baseball cap, a man slumped against the other side of the glass. It had started raining.

Paul?

What's that? he said.

Do I qualify for the job?

Kid, what's the rush?

I don't mean to push you—

Sure, you do, he said.

—but I need the cash. Since you said that I, I've waited tables two months, so I was hoping . . .

He dropped his pen on the pulpit top. Tell me something, he said. Do I look like I give a fuck what you need?

No.

He nodded. On the third upswing, he raised his head. Do I care what you need, or what I need?

What you need, Paul.

I'll ask you something, he said. Why do people sit down at a restaurant like this, make a night of it? It's not the food. If all they want is to eat, they can drive half a mile to the closest shop, buy a big, filling roast fucking chicken for six bucks. It's not this crowd. Who spends to line up at the trough with a pile of strangers to get fed in unison like pigs? No. They're wild about a first-rate place like this because it's selling an illusion.

He paused, expecting a response. It's an illusion, I recited.

That's it, he said. Illusions, kiddo—but of what?

The illusion of love, I said. I'd overheard him giving this catechism to waiters before. He clapped my back.

Bingo. To be fed well is also to feel loved. But like with all illusions, you've got to be consistent. This cousin of mine, he worked in Disneyland, and he dressed up like one of those animals, Mickey, Ducky, I forget. His one job, it's to strut around, let the little kids take pictures with him. They'd shout like he was this big hero. Not so hard, right? But then one day he felt sick, so he took off his head to throw up, and this one kid who noticed, he lost his shit. See, the kid believed my cousin was the cartoon. From the kid's angle, Mickey had ripped off his own head. Like that, my cousin lost his job. Why? Because he busted the illusion. His boss told him, Idiot, you should have thrown up *in* your costume. Will, at times, I look at you, I can tell you're not faking it right. I want you to act like this place is a magic kingdom. Do you get what I'm saying?

I said I did. He picked up his gold pen again. The first diners traipsed in, a trio of women collapsing rain-slick umbrellas. The host assigned them to my section. Writing down drink orders, I considered Paul's speech. He wasn't criticizing my table-waiting abilities. Otherwise, I wouldn't still have this job, let alone the night shift. But I should try acting more like him, I thought. Slap backs as he did, dispersing jokes, high spirits. It's often all people want, urging a change: be like me, shaped in this image.

Guests blew in from the street, wind-spun, gasping for alcohol. They ate, paid, and left, fast, letting the tables go. It worked to my benefit, but I didn't understand people who finished, then rushed out. If I'd paid to eat at a restaurant like Michelangelo's, I'd dawdle. I'd sip a tall limoncello, let waiters refill the glass. I was about to drop a five-top's check when the pinstriped man in my section's last open table stopped me. His wife had questions about the veal chop. Of course, I said. The kitchen had run low on the dish, a point I emphasized. If he wished to have it, I should put in the order as soon as possible.

Instead, he elicited details about the preparation while his wife flipped through the wine list, silk dress pleats glinting. I'd have liked to watch how light played on the gas-blue of the dress. The left dress strap pulled taut across the dip of the woman's collarbone like a bridge traversing a ravine, and one could imagine following its arched, liquid line, sliding a hand back, down until the first swell of buttocks—but I had a job to do. I kept my attention on the man as I answered his questions.

If I say I want it rare, is that something your chef will give me? he asked.

Yes, sir, he——

I can't eat veal that isn't rare.

You'll hear it bleat.

With that, he smiled. I took down his orders, but once I made a trip to the kitchen, I had to return to apologize. Someone else had claimed the last available chop.

Is that right? he said. Extending a lightly muscled arm across the table, in a gesture more languid than alarmed, his wife moved a painted fingertip along the top of his hand, from the wrist to his third knuckle joint. He inhaled. I want to talk to Paul, he said, lowering his voice. He's a friend of mine. Go tell Paul that Miles Harris says hello. He'll recognize the name.

I'm sorry, sir, but Mr. Conti isn't here.

I thought I saw him. Is he gone for the night? You should tell him that putting an item on his menu, then not having it——it's false advertising, which isn't legal.

I nodded. I let him talk. Paul was downstairs, in his office. If this man had been his friend, I'd have known it by now. When I could, I apologized again. I offered cocktails, gratis; I mentioned the suckling-pig ravioli, the Michelin critic who'd extolled Michelangelo's poached quail. I convinced him to substitute the quail for veal, but when I brought him the martinis he sent them back. I fetched a second round; he told me to wait. His round lips parted for the rill of clear liquid. He took more sips. The drink's fine, he said, but I'll switch waiters.

I misheard him, I thought. But there was no mistaking his satisfied face, the gin-wetted lips widening with a grin. I'll find someone else, I said. I turned away, but not before he muttered to his wife. She chortled. It was the first time she'd emitted a sound. I found Isabel, one of the other waiters, frothing hot milk into a tin. I asked if she could take the table. I'm falling behind, I explained.

She looked up from the machine, surprised. I have a full section, too, she said.

Please, Isabel, I said. She'd trained me during my first week here, and still passed along helpful hints. Push the branzino. That three-top tips badly. Watch out for Paul tonight. I tried to keep a light tone, but I hoped she knew I wouldn't have asked if it weren't urgent. I took the foamed milk; I poured it into the waiting cups. I'll owe you, I said.

She shook her head. Earrings swiveled, thin feathers. Sure, all right, she said. I returned to the other tables, but what had been an even, yielding night lost its swing and give. I fell behind. I dropped wine-bloodied napkins. Though I listed specials or balanced plates, I kept hearing the wife's laugh. Then, standing up, a man pushed back into my shins. Careful, he said, as if I'd shoved into him.

I apologized. I went to the bathroom, leaned on the sink.

The basin burned white in the glass. No loss occurs in isolation, and a side profit of the faith that I missed at times like this was how easily, while Christ shone in each face, I loved. If hatred cuts both ways, to forgive can be a balm, and I often missed, as I would a friend, the more tranquil person I now had no reason to be.

I opened the spigot. I washed my hands, then face; eyes closed, I saw my mother wringing out long, baptized hair, twisting it into a rope. Released, the strands flew loose, flicking wet silt. She picked me up, my legs swinging. I thought I felt His elation in her hold, glimpsed it in the silt-sparked light. I used to love imagining His hand upon me, its heft and size: I'd known His impress in the laddering of my ribs, His fingerprint in the whorl crowning my head. The God I followed had been as real to me as a living person—more real, since I'd put so much into inventing Him.

In time, they'd all want me to explain how I lost my faith. John Leal, the others—they kept asking, and I'd recognize the fascination. Scripture indicates there's no hope for the apostates, like me: having known His love, then repudiated Him, I'm believed to be past saving. I exist beyond His grace. But I tried: will that count for anything, Lord? In the final lists You won't compile, allotting a life that You can't give because, in failing to exist, You've left us behind.

I'd returned from the Beijing mission trip split with doubt, unable to sleep. I begged His help. It was as I'd told Phoebe. I had no single problem, or quibble; the misgivings had piled up, questions I stifled as long as I could. The last hours I believed, I'd knelt, asking for a sign. He'd assisted others. Old Testament prophets, along with all the pastors who heard God talk. Friends exulting about His presence. This much love, I thought, must have its match in truth. I'd asked Him to help, then waited. Sunlight spilled in from the afternoon. White curtains rippled, a slight late-spring wind. I waited, and by the time I got up I knew I'd been pleading with no one.

I dried my hands, and I left the bathroom. I was taking dishes into the kitchen when Paul grabbed my arm. The two-top at table nine, he said, his hard stomach bumping my hip. Give me an update, kid. Tell me there isn't an issue.

I started explaining, but Paul interrupted. I don't get it, he said. If the kitchen was low, why'd you push the veal?

I didn't. He asked about it, so—

But he took the fucking quail. Why didn't you push the bird from the start?

It was a valid question. I knew he had a camera that fed live footage from the dining room to his office; Paul, who missed nothing, would of course have noticed a patron throwing a fit, so why hadn't I prepared a better explanation? I'd seen him fire people for less.

Well, I said, he showed up wanting veal. He's been here before, said he's a friend. Miles Harris. But, ah, he asked me to tell you he thinks it's false advertising to run out of dishes we have on the menu, and that false advertising is illegal. He said it's a lie.

He told you I'm lying.

No, the menu, I said. He called the menu a lie.

So, who writes this menu, then? Just who talks with Joel to come up with the dishes? Miles Harris. Who the fuck does he think he is? If we were back in the old country, I'd take him out to the street. We'd settle the question of who's lying.

The kitchen had fallen silent, or what passes for silence in an active kitchen: knife-thuds, rattled pots. Hot oil skittering, the slap of trout hitting steel. The stove's high ping. Paul, being dishonest, hated to be told he'd lied. No one could have said, for instance, which old country belonged to him. He wasn't Italian; he claimed to be since, he said, it helped his business. Real, my ass, he liked saying. Each fucking dish you'll purchase in America, if it's French, Thai, top-flight, it's all made by diligent-as-hell illegals. Mexicans. You've got a Colombian, maybe a Dominican. That's it. But people don't want you to talk like this. They like you to choke up while you tell them about childhood frolics with the Italian grandma who rolled out tortellini dough. So, that's what I am, I'm Italian American. If anyone asks, I piss Sicilian sunlight. I shit big, beautiful oranges.

Six, a chef called out. It was my table. I should take that, I said.

Write down for me the little man's name, Paul said. I want it in my records.

I will.

Who's that with him? I mean, what's a good-looking girl like that doing with a fuck like him?

She's his wife, I said.

Like hell she is. In that dress. Where's your sense, kiddo? If she's his wife, I'm his pop.

A muscle pulsed in his jaw; the entire kitchen was listening. Magic kingdoms, I thought, then I let him have what he wanted.

Maybe you're right, I said. He might have paid for the privilege of the girl's time.

He nodded, half-closing his eyes. Fits with his taste for young meat, he said.

It's no surprise he got upset.

Think it's more like a long-term setup, or like a one-night thing?

Oh, long term, I said. I heard the woman's laugh again, its ripple of satisfaction. For him, I said, she's like a veal calf. He'll keep her caged until she's ripe.

With that, he hooted, hitting his thigh. Others had joined in, providing still more parallels between livestock and girls, when I spotted Isabel in front of the swing doors. One night, she'd admitted she had trouble being the single female hire. They're always talking about bitches and putas, she said. In principle, I agreed; until now, I hadn't added to this kind of machismo, but what could I do? The walk-in hissed open. I glanced at Isabel again. With a flap of white earrings, she left the kitchen.

I carried the plates to my table. I saluted fresh arrivals. By the time I returned to the kitchen, people had started shouting out bets on the Harris wife's alleged price. Paul had appointed himself the betting-pool judge, and all those permitted inside the dining room found an excuse to stroll past the veal aficionado's wife. Dishwashers thronged with line chefs into Paul's office to examine his live feed. Bets got one-upped, cash flung down. The final purse came to more than nine hundred dollars. Let's make it an even grand, Paul said, throwing in extra bills. He called the price. A waiter, Josh, won the pool. While he crowed, I asked if I could borrow a little cash.

Man, just take it, he said, thrusting a fistful of his winnings into my apron pocket. I promised I'd pay him back, but he declined, laughing. You made this jackpot happen, he said.

———

Shift ending, I locked myself in the bathroom to count the night's take. With what Josh had lent me, and what I'd make in the next shift, I'd have enough. I'd deposit the cash Friday morning. I riffled the soft pile of bills. The week after the Beijing trip, I'd returned from class to find my mother unconscious, holding an emptied pill bottle. I called an ambulance; while she was still in the hospital, in the psychiatric ward, the house's water had been suspended. I hadn't seen a final notice about the bill, but when I twisted the tap knob, nothing happened. She'd be released from the hospital in three days. If I didn't fix the situation in time, I'd have failed again. I hit the useless faucet, but then I called the utilities help line. I negotiated. I explained. I paid what I could, and I had it all working before she came home.

When I left the restaurant, I saw Isabel. I asked what she was doing.

I have a ride coming.

I'll wait with you, I said, until it's here. She objected, so I insisted. It was late, the street deserted. It's not safe, I said.

Do as you like, she said, turning aside. She fidgeted with a phone. I took out mine. I'd hoped to apologize, but Isabel's play-acted silence, this hostile charade—she didn't know how much I needed the cash. It wasn't as though I had a choice. The asphalt, still wet, shone with the night. A pickup truck fishtailed to the curb, and Isabel hurried in.

11.

JOHN LEAL

He'd heard the stories. While attending a freshman rooftop party, in defiance of the potential eleven-story fall, Phoebe had walked the ledge with both arms out, like an aerialist. She lived as if spotlit, each laugh evidential, loud. He asked around: she hadn't told friends what she'd lost. But all this, he could use. The public fronts people held up showed him as much, if not more, as the factual selves. He often thought of a time his gulag had received an aid shipment, boxes of nail polish. It was the first time he saw the female prisoners energized. They traded food rations, clothes, to obtain the cosmetic; they painted their nails a vital red. Though frozen, starving, they still wished to feel desirable. In a lifetime, the average woman will eat her weight in lipstick. To covet is to begin to have. The ancients had believed the soul lived in the stomach, coeval with its appetite. The girl had walked the high-dive ledge as if she couldn't die.

12.

I'm still not telling it right, though, Phoebe said: all through my disciplined childhood, I fantasized about having the time to do nothing. Now that I had time, the hours felt like a wasteland. I crossed it, back and forth. Old ambitions flopped like stranded fish. Inside, the Phoebe I'd been still flailed. I hadn't come to Edwards to attend all its parties, but I avoided being alone. While out, with friends, I could live as they did. Oh, people here tried to be polite; raised well, they had etiquette driving them; but I, desperation. If I asked the first question, then if I listened, head tilted, providing attention, they let me ask again. Punctilios forgotten, they prattled along. They'd tell me everything. Julian, for instance, had parents who hadn't talked to him in months.

In months, I said. What—why—

They don't believe sexual orientation exists, he said. So, they think I'm being selfish, that I'm staging a quick rebellion. I lived at a friend's place once I graduated high school, to get away from them. If they were less Korean, they'd stop paying my tuition, but the only thing they'd find more humiliating than being saddled with a homosexual child is a homosexual, college-dropout child.

His voice cracked, splitting open; but, just then, his friend Liesl Ruhl leaned down from the daybed where she'd been dozing. Face paint had bled lawn-green onto an outfit of white bridal tulle, lace rags tied with ribbon bits. Tattered leaves pinned a veil to Liesl's head. She flicked Julian's arm. I want a refill, she said.

The drinks are in the kitchen, Liesl.

But *Julian*—

I stood. I'll get it, I said. I need a drink, too.

I found wine; I poured two large portions, then a third, in case Julian wanted his own. Hands full, I picked a path through the paint-stained, strewn bodies of Liesl's cast. It was the play's final night. In ripped tulle, howling, actors had flitted across the blacklit stage. They pelted the back wall with vines, then fell in piles. I still wasn't sure what I'd seen; when I asked Julian if he could fill me in, he whispered, Believe me, it's my third time watching this, oh, exhibit, and I've quit raising questions. I've filed it with all the world's riddles that lack solutions. What's life, and so forth.

I sat down with Julian and his friend again. Liesl lifted a mottled face, the veil lopsided. I adore you, she said, taking the glass. She leaned forward; when she settled back, the costume slipped to the side. Panties showed: a strip of cloth, flashing red. Julian readjusted the lace rags. Underpants, angel, he said. She laughed, jolting the drink.

Jules, tell Phoebe about the time we dressed up the Hale statue, she said.

Oh, Christ, the—

Catgut!

They both doubled up, barely able to talk. In high school, they gasped. It was a stunt they'd pulled. This recollection led to others, old tales, boarding-school hijinks, but it was all right. I laughed along. Julian, tired, slid down, leaning his head on my thigh. I kissed the white line of his part. I'd wait. If for a short while, Julian had split himself open. Now pain, like light, leaked through his cracked surface. Within days, he'd tell me about the brother who died before he was born. I can't live up to him, he'd explain. He's the ideal, this ghoul sibling. Since I exist, I can't help upsetting them.

Liesl licked spilled alcohol from the back of a hand, and I thought of the whine she'd used to tell Julian she wanted a drink, the expectation that he, a man, would hop to her bidding. I once heard him ask Liesl where she learned to manipulate men. Step-fathers, plural, she told him, lifting one side of a thin-lipped mouth as though it were a joke. I hadn't talked much with Liesl, but I would: in time, she'd confide in me, as well. The dad she'd idolized, who left; the men like beads on the string of a furious mother's life. The anorexic spells. She'd been locked up in a clinic. Obliged to eat, to weigh in. Like a pig for the kill, she said.

———

I kept listening. Often, at parties, I could be found in the kitchen, a back porch, eliciting still more troubles. If people cried, I held damp hands. With the squash recruit, too; the ball-pit poet, the flautist; Tim, then Phil, it wasn't lust. Plain lust, I'd have re-spected. Instead, I craved the postcoital talks, the truths told in bed. I ate pain. I swilled tears. If I could take enough in, I'd have no space left to fit my own. In turn, I couldn't walk five minutes through Noxhurst without hearing a dozen hellos. Faces lit up if I walked into a room, the liking a light I could refract, giving it back. Phoebe, oh, I love that girl, people said, but it's possible they all just loved the reflected selves.

(Here's a story she used to tell: once, I drank a bottle of my mother's perfume while she was out of town. I was little, still too young to believe such a long absence could be revoked. So, I chased down what I did have, the love I'd lost distilled in scent.

It worked, though, my mother would explain, laughing. When Haejin opened her eyes, I was there. I'd rushed to the hospital. They'd pumped the child's stomach. I didn't leave Haejin with anyone else for years.)

Will, at first, was like the others. I was at a party again, dancing, when I spotted him. He stood next to the alcohol, his face a stranger's. By this point, a month since I'd come to Edwards, I thought I'd met all the partiers. He held his plastic cup to his mouth a long while, his solitude obvious. It pulled me in. I shifted into his line of vision, but he kept looking past me, into the crowd of bodies. He lifted his drink again. Fine, I thought. I had a half-cup full of punch. Foam sloshed, poison red. Still dancing, I moved close to him. I tipped the cup, letting punch spill down his leg.

13.

WILL

I'd felt, for months, as though I lived pushed up against glass walls. I couldn't find a way in. Out on the sidewalk, alone, I watched the crowds reveling inside. With Phoebe, the walls lifted. Invitations spilled out; warmth, life. I also pledged a fraternity, Phi Epsilon, when I heard about its influential alumni, the class portraits lined with well-known faces. I wasn't eating enough, but at parties, in the Phi Epsilon house, alcohol was plentiful. I drank more. Still, I kept my grades high. I barely slept; I wanted every prize. I intended to outdo all these people I lied to imitate, the lotus-eaters who sprawled on the lawn. I finished the last final exam, an evening class, then I stumbled home. I fell in bed. I planned to celebrate with Phoebe at the Colonial, but instead, when I opened my eyes again, I saw that mild light filled the room. It was late morning. I'd slept through the night. I called Phoebe: she was on the train, going to the airport.

I came by your suite when I didn't hear from you, she said. If Julian hadn't left for Berlin, I'd have recruited him to pick the lock. I kept calling. I heard your phone from out on the landing. I should have just let you sleep, but I wanted to see you—

I spent most of the break in ice-piled Noxhurst, working extra shifts at the restaurant. In late fall, Paul had finally given me a promotion; I couldn't have left during the holiday rush. I thought, too, that I should save a little cash while I had the time. I helped see Michelangelo's through New Year's Eve, an upheaval of white-peach Bellinis and smashed flutes, banderoles and tricolored spumoni (a Conti tradition, I heard Paul tell a table), then I flew home to Carmenita.

It was the first trip back since I'd started school. I'd anticipated the pleasure I'd see on my mother's face, but then, almost as soon as the plane landed, I wanted to leave again. Outlines softened, salt in liquid; I felt how easily I could dissolve into the life I'd left behind. Ripped flip-flops still held the stain of old footprints. She asked me to attend church. I said I couldn't; I offered to drive, past the graffiti-blotched traffic signs I didn't need to consult. I let her out, then left in a rush to evade old friends who, still God-wild, pitied me. Radio stations I'd left preset hadn't changed. Last spring, while she was being held captive in the hospital, I avoided the house. Instead, I'd taken to driving around town at night to look in at people's lives. Intact families sat in the blue wash of television light, tranquil, like drowned statues.

I noticed, too, that she'd kept up the habit of red lipstick, the starlet's hue my father used to like. He insisted she put it on, this high-effort cosmetic: she had to check it often, making sure it hadn't bled. She wasn't an attention-getting woman. Bold red was his preference, not hers. Each time she applied it, she might as well have been signaling across the miles that she still loved him.

I talked as often as I could to Phoebe. She'd grown up in L.A., and though I'd made it up, perhaps because, I felt that this shared childhood belonged more to me. It was the upbringing she'd received by chance, while I'd picked mine: I cultivated it, and kept it alive. In fact, at first, I resented Phoebe's theft of citrus trees and jasmine, the tennis balls whirling in full sunlight. But she accepted what I said without question; now, isolated as I felt, Phoebe's belief helped me recall who I could be. By this point, we'd had to be apart almost a month. Phone calls spun out hours at a time. She was in Berlin with Julian, visiting his boyfriend, Sunil. I drifted into sleep with the phone hot at my face, Phoebe's voice like a song.

Will, we didn't get back to Sunil's place until 10:00 in the morning. It's so bright in his living room that I can't sleep except with a shawl tied around my head. Julian says that, even if he's drunk, *when*, I can't let him ask Sunil to quit his Berlin experi-

ment. I broke a heel last night, dancing. Julian said I wasn't allowed to go home. That, as his closest friend, I was obligated to
stay with him. He tore his shirt, instead. He tied the cloth rags
on my feet, like booties. Dancing slippers.

———

It was around this time that she first told me her mother had
died, along with how it happened: that she, Phoebe, had been
driving, unused to cars. I didn't know how to respond. I'm so
sorry, Phoebe, I said, at last.

No, I just, I haven't told people at Edwards, she said. I refuse
to be the sad girl, with people whispering, but—I've known you
awhile. I wanted to tell you. Well, I've told Julian. John Leal also
knows, but that was my father's doing. It's life. Let's talk about
something else.

———

I did think, during this break, to look him up online. I found a
couple of local-interest articles, Edwards *Herald* squibs. John
Leal, so I learned, while he was still a student, had gotten into a
late-night fistfight with a Noxhurst local, one so violent that
he'd been jailed. No charges had been pressed; John Leal, released. It looked as though the college had then suspended him.
Expelled, perhaps: I couldn't find him listed with his graduating

class. The more recent article featured protests he organized with local churches. He'd marshaled a pro-life group that knelt each morning in front of the local women's clinic, Phipps. It was the largest abortion-providing clinic in New York. Jo was mentioned; Ian, too. I told Phoebe what I learned, but she didn't sound interested. Of all the futile causes, she said. She hadn't seen him, not since he'd invited us to his house.

———

During the fall term, I'd applied for a part-time Edwards research position with David Ling, a Nobel-lauded economist. It paid less than waiting tables, but it would, of course, help me with future jobs. I started working with him when I returned to Noxhurst, and I lived through a week of trying to do both before I realized I had to cut back at Michelangelo's. The night I planned to tell Paul, he pitched a deboned tilapia fillet at a line cook's head. Missing its target, the fish hit the wall, then slid down, trailing oil. It fell to the linoleum, slumped into its tail. I was going to be fired, I thought.

But instead, when I told Paul I had no choice but to work less, he asked if this meant I was giving notice. If you're quitting on me, you little shit, I'll have your balls, he said. I'll wrap them up like quail eggs. I'll tie on a blue ribbon to match, I'll send them compliments of Paul Conti to—

No, I just need to cut down my hours. I'll find someone to fill in.

More insults followed, but he sounded tired, listless, as though forced to recite old lines. Christ, all right, he said, as long as he didn't notice the change. Once home, I pulled out a bottle of gin. I finished the first glass, and I was pouring a second when I heard the rush of footsteps. Phoebe swept in, jingling the keys I'd had copied. She held a paint-striped mask; a floor-length cape swung and trailed around her legs. I've come straight from a costume party, she said. In Liesl's suite. It was so hot, but I kept the mask on until I left. I think I should get a prize. No one except Julian could figure out who I was.

What did you tell them?

That I'm the queen of Tajikistan. I abdicated the throne to enroll here.

Tajikistan, I said. I don't think it has a queen.

Will, that's my *point*.

She'd brought an opened bottle of champagne, which she tipped into the nearest cup. Froth dribbled onto the torn gold label. That's for you, she said, unzipping salt-stained boots. She kissed me, tongue flickering in my mouth. With a laugh, she broke free. I was talking in a big circle of people, she said. But then, I thought, What the hell am I doing? I want to be with Will.

She listed, taking a half-spin. I helped Phoebe lie down. I forgot to be careful. She asked what I was up to, and I said, I'm celebrating. I've settled the problem with the restaurant: I found a solution Paul can live with—

What restaurant? Who's Paul?

Even then, I still could have fixed the mistake. But in the low-wattage lamplight, Phoebe's face was shining. It floated like a reflection, detached, the pale, thin shape I knew as I did my own. I'm tired of lying, I said. I explained about Paul. I waited tables at a place called Michelangelo's. Each time I claimed to be in a library carrel, I'd had to go to the restaurant. I didn't have a carrel. I studied at home. She'd known about my mother's illness, the pills; I'd told Phoebe my father left us while I was on a mission trip to Beijing, but now I outlined what had followed. The financial problems. Debt; going bankrupt. Double-shift nights. The profound shame of owing money in a small town. I talked about Carmenita. The first minutes on campus, when I saw the sunlit lawn unrolled.

I've wanted to tell you, I said. I didn't know how to explain. I'd have told you the truth from the start if I'd known I, sometimes I thought you guessed, but you—

No, you don't—

—too considerate, or—

Will, don't fucking pretend I was in on this.

That's not what I'm saying.

The fact that you lied to me for months instead of telling me where you're from—

She zipped on her boots, then left. I called, but she didn't pick up; I left messages, apologizing. The next morning, when I went to Phoebe's suite, she refused to let me in. I went home. I waited. I stared at the ceiling, unable to sleep. I tried a sedative, prescribed at the student clinic. It had no effect. Drunks traversed the quadrangle, the shouts and songs echoing through closed glass. I should get up, I thought, but then Phoebe stood across the lawn in a gilded dress. Pale limbs, exposed, were gleaming. But aren't you chilled, I wanted to ask. The crowd swelled. Phoebe, I called, frantic, trying to keep the girl in sight. In spite of the cold, they all stripped down. Carnival masks blossomed in the field of skin; bodies mingled, and then I woke up again. The days lengthened, inflating into a full week alone, without Phoebe. Each night, I attended parties. I hoped she'd be there. Once, I thought I glimpsed Phoebe leaving the dining hall with a man who looked like John Leal, the brushed-up cockerel's plume flaunting high above his head. By the time I pushed through the Wyeth portico, I'd lost them.

I don't know how long she'd have kept silent if, one night, as I walked to the bus stop for a shift, I hadn't glanced up and noticed Phoebe in front of me, a half-block down. She paused in front of a coffee-shop storefront, reflected beneath the Café Azul sign: she might have been a levitating ghost, superimposed on the people inside. She wore a coat open, with a long slit down the back. I lifted a hand; I held my breath, afraid to wave. She turned, then walked to me. The beige coat halves rose, floating behind bared legs.

I'm sick of being apart, she said. But if it happens again, I'll—

It won't, I said.

She was shaking, the sharp features flushed. I held Phoebe; I kissed what I could reach. Is it only in hindsight that I notice an isolated figure at the end of the street, watching us, or does the clarity with which I see him outlined in faint light prove it's a fiction? Each time I've reviewed what I've kept of this evening, I'm less sure. I know, though, how he liked to plan. But that night, I made nothing of it. The slope of Phoebe's neck was hot, sweat-humid. If it happens, she started saying. With a kiss, I stalled the threat; I shut Phoebe's mouth with mine.

14.

JOHN LEAL

Noxhurst, though, his group said. Of all the places he could have gone after Yanji, why had he returned here, to his old college town? But John Leal saw no need to indulge such questions. He'd had his troubles, it was true. The night he first left Noxhurst, he'd imagined he'd never return. I've since learned, he might have said, that nothing energizes like humiliation. It had rained his first day out of the gulag, the lines slanting like marionette strings. In each breath he inhaled, he'd heard the call of the dying Christ. But none of this merited saying. It would be weak to tell too much, to explain. It could mislead. The Lord eludes the whys. To insist is also a slight; give me, we plead, testing Him. In pursuit, we misprize. Lord, increase my bewilderment, they'd do well to ask. Instead, he told them he had been called back to Noxhurst, God wanting him here. Just as He wants all of you, he said, looking in turn at his disciples' upturned faces.

15.

PHOEBE

Up at the Point, Phoebe said, Will and I lolled on full bellies. Toy-sized, a plane pitched along the horizon. It dipped then rolled, playful. I watched a coin of light slip down his chin. It was the fifth date in as many days; late the previous night, as we walked home, he'd asked if I liked picnics. If so, I'll plan it, he said. He brought all the food. Stilton hunks, fat-pebbled pâté. Plum jam. The half-baguette. Ripe peaches. Mulled wine in a jug.

I ate too much, past appetite. It would be months before Will admitted he was broke, and I couldn't have known he'd paid for this banquet, with its pâté, the out-of-season fruit, using tips he couldn't spare. Still, it was obvious he'd put in effort. The first night I met him, for instance, I'd talked about craving a good peach. To mull this wine, he'd stolen into the dining-hall kitchen.

I tried to slice the fruit. The knife slipped, cutting my left hand. I winced. It was a small cut, but he insisted on tying a folded napkin around it. Here, he said. I let him have the paring knife. With his large, blunt-nailed hands, he sliced the peach. He didn't ask how I lacked this basic skill. I held the first piece to his mouth, and he bit into it. White flesh dribbled juice. Before I could wipe off the liquid, he kissed my wrist clean.

(I had no practice slicing fruit because my mother had always done it, bringing plates heaped with Fuji apples to the piano room: a fork, too, so that I could practice without dirtying my hands. I nibbled slices between scales, the late-afternoon sun oiling the top of my head like a benediction, a sign of grace. If I then tried to clean the dish, she didn't let me. Haejin, go practice, she said.)

Too full to eat more, I pointed out the plane. He raised his head, obedient; he looked up. I'd love to learn how to do that, he said. To fly a plane. Just in case.

In case . . .

If, mid-flight, the pilot fainted, or—

But planes have two pilots.

Not small planes.

Right, I said. So, on this little plane, if the pilot fainted, you'd hurtle into the cockpit. You'd save lives, the big hero.

That's right, he said, laughing. I touched the tip of my nose to his. I wasn't sure, though, what I was doing. Oh, I'd gained his attention: from the moment I spilled punch on his thigh, and he turned to find me smiling up at him, I'd had it, him. I'd chat-ted, then started dancing. He lifted one shoe at a time, inept. I'm not used to this, he said. I adjusted my tempo to his, following his motions until, relaxing, he twitched his limbs; he tried to spin me in a circle. I let him. I liked how he looked at me, as if he couldn't help it.

But since then, five nights ago, I persisted in spending time with him. Our legs mingled beneath the thick plaid blanket he'd also thought to bring. His toes pressed my calves. I hadn't taken him to bed; I kept waiting. I didn't think I should treat him like a one-night fling. Days passed, then weeks. He proved more evasive than even I could be. He joshed and hid. I sighted him in flashes. Late one night, while talking about religious faith, Liesl had said, I'd love to believe there's something out there. It's hard to imagine this is all, then we die.

What solid logic, Will said. Top-notch wishful thinking.

He tried to smile, as if he'd told a joke. Liesl, no idiot, winced. I filled the silence that followed by talking about the time when, as a kid, reaching for a mall-fountain nickel, I'd fallen in. Before long, I had everyone laughing; afterward, when Julian alluded to Will's bad mood, I acted as though I hadn't noticed. Oh, please, Julian said. But he hadn't seen the twist in Will's smile, how pitiful he looked. Such bravado, like a small child taught he'd be punished if he cried. From the little he let slip about leaving his church, I tried to conceive of what he'd lost. The high-minded world he used to inhabit: ordered, calm.

I didn't think I'd die, he said. It's a fringe benefit of the faith. I believed I'd always live, along with everyone I loved.

I wished I could ask how he'd survived giving up so much. But in general, he avoided talking about life as a Christian. He'd joke; otherwise, he pushed it to the side. With me, too, once I told him about my mother's death, he shied from bringing it up. It was like high school, after the crash, when even close friends had failed to ask about it: afraid, I think, to remind me I was grieving. They hadn't known it wasn't possible, since I didn't, at any point, forget.

Instead, Will hustled. He strove. It felt as though, having lost the infinite, he couldn't waste what little time he had. On piled Post-its, to-do lists proliferated. He brushed his teeth while underlining Plotinus. If he had to watch a film for class, he fit in dumbbell lifts, as well. He walked fast, then studied past dawn.

But he also slowed his pace to mine. During the college tricentennial parade, while people with blue flags pushed down Whiting Street, he kept his arm circling my shoulders, firm, so that I wouldn't be carried away from him. Unlike most of my Edwards friends, he could be depended upon. If he said he'd do something, he did it; if he promised to meet me at a specific time, he was there. He liked to help. To fix. The tap dripped in my suite bathroom. I said I'd call the Edwards service line, but Will, wielding pliers, solved it first. He'd been an Eagle Scout. Still am, he said. He'd kitted out a survival go-bag with basic supplies, stashing it beneath his bed: iodine tablets, a wind-up flashlight. Rubbing alcohol. Packs of food. Within a month, he zipped provisions in for me, as well. But I still didn't feel, or want, as he did.

When we did start having sex—less, perhaps, because I wanted to, than to please him—he often slept with a hand cupping my head, as if to protect me from bad dreams. In his tranquil face, I could picture the stolid kid he'd have been, reliable, walking to his bedridden mother with a glass full of milk—

Toddling, I'd have said. I used to imagine him toddling with the glass brimful of milk, holding it in his boy's hands, but this wasn't right. He'd enrolled in his Bible college by then. If I were less selfish, I'd have released the hold I had on him, this love-dazed Will, more child than man. But I wasn't. I couldn't. He took the stairs to my suite at a full run. Bruises formed at the tops of my thighs. If I went to bed after he did, Will turned toward me, still asleep. I might put my head next to his, but he'd clamp his hot legs around mine. He hauled me in. I tried not to pull loose; still, I did. He protested. Insistent, not quite conscious, he reached for me again. I listened to his pulse. His soft, thin hairs, dandelion strands, shifted between my lips. I breathed them in. Here's a wish, I thought. Don't let me go. Until Will, I drifted: he attached me to this patch of earth. He clung all night.

16.

WILL

In June, I went to Beijing for a paid internship at a small investment fund. The plan had included Phoebe, who said she'd come along. But then, in the spring, she was advised she risked failing. Unless she improved a grade or two, she'd be forced to take remedial summer classes.

I asked what I could do, and she pulled open the plastic that sealed still-pristine textbooks. She started attending lectures. I tried to help, but if discipline is a muscle, hers had atrophied. Old habits revived. She slept past noon, ignoring class. Instead, she spilled time into high-profile stunts: the Presidential House break-in, for instance. To plan it, she joined a guided visit of the house. She photographed walls, slid open a ground-level window bolt. With the help of Liesl, who acted in college shows, she pillaged the Playhouse supplies closet for matching clothes. She held a photo shoot. Invited to participate, I told Phoebe I didn't have the time. She used the pictures she'd taken in his house to stage the president's familial portraits. Her friends modeled poses, replicating facial expressions. The next time President Wright left town, they stole into his house, and switched his photos with their own. The *Herald* published a short, admiring tribute.

It shouldn't have come as a surprise, then, when Phoebe learned she had to remain in Noxhurst. But I'd been hopeful. I'd already accepted the Beijing job, a position Ling had helped me find. I'd put down the deposit on a Shichahai apartment; the bank had purchased my round-trip flights.

No, you're going, Phoebe said, when I proposed I'd find a substitute job in Noxhurst: I could work at Michelangelo's, for instance. Will, three months isn't that long. I'll visit you.

But you'll be alone.

I'll have friends here.

Who? I said.

If anything, Julian will be in the city. I'll go see him. I'll meet people. They'll love me. People do.

What about, ah, I said, but I hesitated. Damp spring wind blew in. I inhaled the lazy, bittersweet stink that lingered in her room from a hyacinth bouquet she'd let spoil in a vase. I'd thrown it out, but the rich hint of rot persisted. Is Liesl—

No, Julian said she'll be home. In St. Paul.

I still didn't know Liesl well; Phoebe had mentioned, though, that she'd also been directed to enroll in remedial classes. Then, in April, she'd filed a rape charge against the New York governor's son, Neil Pugh. Details of the night had since become public: a full living room, the tall girl following him up the stairs. Not everyone believed Liesl. I knew Neil, a little. He'd joined Phi Epsilon in the spring, then dropped out. Neil, a sailing recruit, looked the part: disheveled, wind-blown, as if he'd always just strolled off a boat. Despite the Nantucket reds he affected, his ripped twilled shirts, he'd lived most of his life in San Francisco, in his divorced mother's house. It was a short drive from Carmenita. I avoided him, as a result; despite the distance I kept, if not because of it, he'd invited me to several parties. Poor girl, I said.

Before long, Phoebe was taking me to the airport, and it was too late to shift course. We parted at the curb, brusque: we'd argued that morning. I called when I landed in Beijing. She apologized, so I did, as well, both each other's old selves again, and while we talked about schedules, plotting phone dates, I could almost believe Phoebe to be within reach and not, as she was, divided from me by miles of land and sea.

The job at the fund turned out to be more tiring than I'd expected. I worked long hours. Often, I had to cancel phone calls with Phoebe. The first time I stayed the night at the office, napping thirty minutes beneath a desk in the morning, colleagues hailed me as if I'd been admitted to an exclusive club.

It surprised me, how much I liked the work. I could be confident in the finance demimonde, with its upstart cowboy strut, its practitioners bloated with the hubris of men—and it was all men—paid well at high-profile jobs. The hum of competence filled the office, like air-conditioning. I built intricate, mazelike financial models, reveling in the fiction of a predictable world. The models multiplied, breeding hypothetical yuan.

I found I enjoyed Beijing, as well. The last time I'd been here, striving to bring locals to Jesus, I hadn't seen it for itself. Rubble had swirled beneath the crush of shoes. I'd thrust illicit Christian brochures into passing hands. I coughed more than I could preach. Now, I had something valid to contribute: I felt big, as if I mattered. In physical fact, I was tall in Beijing. My stride extended long and tireless, a champion's pace, fit for taking spoils, sizing land. Even in bed, my feet hung off the edge. While my head butted the dollhouse ceiling, the city built new towers that pushed against the skies.

There was also the food. In Beijing, I put on weight. I was fed at the office, but then, when I left, I kept eating. For the first time since I lived in Carmenita, I always had enough to eat. I glutted myself on roasted Peking duck and paper-wrapped trout, mapo tofu and thrice-cooked bacon. Boiled, succulent jiaozi. Lamb shish kebabs. Mouth-stinging Sichuan hotpots. Baozi. Jianbing.

Spiced grass carp. I thought of the meals I skipped in Noxhurst. When my pants tightened, I undid a button. I ate more.

But this calm had its limits. Beijing was hot, its inhabitants loud. Used as I was to the quiet of Noxhurst, I couldn't stop noticing the Beijing traffic. In June, I came upon a five-vehicle log-jam pileup. Paramedics hauled bloodstained bodies from twisted cars, and laid them on the asphalt. Blood swelled in slow blooms from splayed limbs. A girl in pale jeans sprawled in a dark pool so vast I had the senseless idea that all the fluids had been pressed out. Cars lunged past, horns wailing, heedless. A motorcyclist's wheel flattened the dead girl's shoe, and kept going.

Then, a fund principal, Martin Phelps, a Brit, hosted an office-wide reception at his house. In spite of the heat, people drifted toward his backyard. His garden, he called it, though he hadn't planted much: the sizable lawn, along with limp floral strands twining up a pergola. He'd placed urns on the grass; tall plinths, too, six of them. Waiters circled with goblet-sized cocktails. I drank fast. The outside lights flicked on. Paper-lantern strings pearled the lawn, like threads drawn tight to unite the crowd, but we all still stood apart. Each guest hovered on his own rising pedestal of late-afternoon shade. The men, in full suits, swabbed napkins across damp faces. Wives swayed in high heels. Thin bracelets tinkled. I listened to a woman cavil about the last trip she'd taken, to a Thai island.

Since I'm, as you can tell, Asian, she said, while Matt, he's white, Thai people kept mistaking me for a bargirl. It's, well, a kind of prostitute. So, one night, the hotel night clerk tried to prohibit me from going in. He shouted at me in Thai. You should have heard Matt yell. It was hilarious.

She laughed, uncertain, then inhaled from a cigarette. Its lit end flared. The tale had fallen flat. If I'd been Phoebe, I'd have replied with tactful questions to help the conversation along. With a light joke, a quick grace note, I'd put this woman, plus all the listeners, at ease. I lacked such skill; instead, I smiled, polite. I excused myself to find a cocktail. It was childish, but I started revising the night. The next time I talked to Phoebe, I'd retell it as the kind of outsize frolic she'd wish she hadn't missed. I'd gild the event, adding the six-piece jazz band, a hired waltzing troupe. Pop champagne to spout, like liquid mirth, from jeroboam bottles. Twirl the partiers. Set them to dance beneath the jasmine, florets dangling like bells from white-limbed pergolas.

The Phelps' house was also in Shichahai, less than a mile from my apartment. I left the party on foot, but I hadn't walked much in Beijing. Within minutes, I was lost. I kept walking. It was a dense, hot night again, the slight wind blood-temperature. Girls on bicycles spun past, black triangle seats wedged between taut buttocks. No one knew where I was in the old, ill-lit alleys, the zigzag streets of the hutong, and not a soul could find me. It seemed the quiet the hermit seeks in the wild or the stylite on his post might be realized here, like this, amid Beijing's chaos. I felt free, blameless: I'd have liked to be lost all night.

Too soon, I happened upon the stalls of street-food hawkers. Steam coiled up in a haze from grills and open pots. I asked for directions at the last cart in my college Mandarin. The peddler replied, but I didn't understand him. The couple waiting in line heard the exchange, and, laughing, said they'd help.

While they sketched a map, I noticed a girl who stopped to purchase food. In the occult light of the hawker's cart, I saw the upturned stub of a nose, a flat bob streaked peacock-blue. She held a translucent plastic backpack with nothing inside. Despite the childish bag, she looked about my age. She had excess baby fat, the kind of flesh a person can grab. Upon receiving the change for a scallion pancake, she inspected the coins, slanting them to the light. Then, she bit into the fried cake; broad front teeth tugged free a long, tantalizing shred of bright green. Inhaling, she sucked both lips clean of oil. She looked nothing like Phoebe, but in relishing the treat, the obvious appetite—it brought my absent girlfriend to mind. We'd fought, again. I hadn't talked to Phoebe in almost a week. She left; I thanked the couple, then I followed the girl.

Staying at half a block's distance, on the opposite side of the street, I kept pace through walled alleys. In the dark, it wasn't hard to keep the girl in sight, the backpack's plastic bulge jolting ahead like a lamp. I tried to walk quietly. Pigeons flapped down, jingling bells tied to their legs. Cyclists passed. I tripped on a pile of bricks. The girl's bob leaped along.

The streets emptied: to keep up, I had to quicken my stride.

She hurried—impatient to be home, I thought; then, turning right, she glanced back. The round face blazing, then gone. Despite the pains I'd taken, she looked afraid. I'd wanted to follow the girl for just a few minutes. But now, accused, I felt insulted.

I saw something white, a sheet, flit from the girl's hand. Thinking it might be a note, a signal, I paused to pick it up, but it was nothing: half the pancake, crumpled into its napkin. I resumed the chase. She doglegged left. I was losing breath. She halted, then bent down. I saw her adjust a sandal strap. She broke into a run, hobbling. Hey, I called. I wanted to explain, so I jogged. With a slam, she rushed into a small house, out of sight.

It was late by the time I returned to the high-rise. I took a pill; I went to bed, but the sedative wasn't working. In Noxhurst, Phoebe would have been next to me, her back displayed, intimate, the spine like rope. I felt tied to her as though by a physical line, its pull tightening with each night we spent apart. Upright again, I put the electric kettle on to boil. I tapped in the first third of Phoebe's number before I set the phone down on the table.

The last time we talked, she'd told me she wasn't coming to Beijing. She'd begun spending time with John Leal again, I knew that much. I'd been right when I thought I glimpsed them in the dining hall. Then, while I was in Beijing, she'd gotten in the habit of attending meetings at his house with the group we met last fall, the Christians. On an impulse, she said. She was bored. Noxhurst was so dull, she said. All this, I'd known; now, though, she was also telling me the group had strict rules about attendance. If she missed meetings to travel to China, she wouldn't be allowed back in.

But what are you even doing with these people? I asked.

These people?

I can't believe this. Who is John Leal—what is he to you?

He's a friend.

You don't know the first thing about him.

I do, though.

Fine, I said. Tell me where he grew up.

In India.

India?

His parents built a charitable hospital in Calcutta.

. . . because they're, what, aid workers?

Will, they're missionaries.

In the pause that followed, hiding I wasn't sure what, I stood in front of the kitchen glass, watching street-level laborers dig. Jackhammers drilled into asphalt. Taxicabs jostled past the ruins, and then they pulled free. I knew that, at some point, I'd left Phoebe with the impression I was hostile to Christians. But what I hadn't explained was that, if I went on a jog, I still heard Leviticus like a song to beat out the rhythm of each stride. If I walked out to a bare street, I panicked—afraid again, until I relearned not to be, that the God in whom I'd stopped believing had lifted His faithful up to His side, leaving the rest of us, who'd declined His pledge, to die. Toward the end, when I felt faith slip from me like the last remnants of a loved, radiant dream, I looked around during church services at all the believing fools, and I grieved with envying them. I used to think I valued truth more than I did the Lord, but I wasn't so heroic. If I could have stayed, I would. It's as though, when I tried to learn His lines by heart, I turned literal. I inked the Word in flesh; I tattooed atrial muscles. It stained the cells, His print indelible. I wasn't hostile, Phoebe. It was longing, and I should have made that plain. Instead, I asked if she'd known all along he'd be in Noxhurst.

What are you implying?

Tell me if that's why you gave up attending classes, I said. If you did this on purpose.

She asked if I heard how I sounded. When had *she* lied to me? Well, all right, I thought, as the kettle pinged. I pulled down a tea bag. Oh, I'd noticed occasional mild deceptions, the milk lies of love, but I hadn't known Phoebe to be dishonest, not like this. But I'd lied so long, I'd found how natural it could be. I let the tea soak. I took a second pill, then I called Phoebe, giving in.

17.

JOHN LEAL

Each time he saw Phoebe, he asked if she could talk to him about the mother who'd died. You're in pain because someone you love has stopped existing, he said. But the love itself is still with you. It's the more abiding gift. She's stayed in this world as she could, through absence. If you can find delight in this lack as you did with presence, you'll gain what you think is lost. But it's hard, he said. Phoebe, it'll take time. He'd lost his mother, too: he'd lived with the resulting isolation. He'd had to learn how it felt to watch others avert their eyes, trying to believe all was well. Is it, though, he asked, until, halting, tearful, she started telling him.

18.

PHOEBE

The wind drifts behind me, Phoebe said. Trash shifts, then I'll find I'm listening to a light footstep, one I almost recognize. Since I don't want to dispel the hope, I'll wait as long as possible before I look back. The truth is, it still feels as though, if I wait long enough, she'll return. I've wondered if I've stopped being able to want, but maybe it's just that what I most wish to have again is not, at this point, available.

19.

WILL

When I finished the job, I returned from Beijing to Noxhurst. In the first flush of reunion with Phoebe, it seemed possible we'd only fought because we'd had to be apart too long. The previous spring, we'd decided to split an apartment; in August, she'd signed the lease on a small place above Café Azul. In bed, in the dining hall, we resisted even short-lived separation. I opened my eyes each morning to find a naked leg thrown across mine, my arm fixed tight across her stomach. I sat through movies I could tell I wouldn't like, just to be at Phoebe's side. While we strolled through campus, she kept a hand tucked in the back pocket of my jeans. The line between us relaxed its hold, the slack winding, like an exhausted snake, at our adjoined feet.

So brazen, Julian said. He raised his full glass to me, then to Phoebe, who leaned into my arm. Did you learn nothing in China, Will? It's such bad luck, flaunting what you've been given. Sensible parents used to insult their own children, calling them idle, stupid—

But less than a month into the term, Liesl took a leave of absence from school. She returned to St. Paul again. The rape allegation had become front-page national news. More Edwards girls had stories to tell of sexual assault. Editorials followed; public outrage. Phoebe helped organize a candlelit vigil, which almost half the school attended. Still, there were students who criticized Liesl, small-minded gossips who prattled about which illegal pills she liked best, how reliable she might be. The possibility she'd lied. Others, less spiteful, said they didn't know what to think. It felt hard to judge Neil outright. In his version, he hadn't touched Liesl. Even friends wanted facts, details. Phoebe, livid, picked late-night quarrels. No one lies about this, she said. Look at what it's cost Liesl, then tell me she's lying.

The next time I went out for the night, she refused to come along. It's fine, go, she insisted. It was a Prohibition costume party; the host, a Phi Epsilon. In ostrich quills, top-hatted, hands chilled from tall glasses clicking ice, people high-fived me, asking about Phoebe.

Where's she hiding? they hollered.

She's staying in.

Is she all *right*?

Yes.

I told Phoebe she'd been missed, that people had asked if she felt ill. I don't care, she said. I fell asleep on the futon, anesthetized with alcohol, but I woke to see her sitting in the open windowsill. Night sounds flowed in while she looked out as if listening for a faint echo—how is Phoebe, how is she—tell us—how is Phoebe. Sometimes, I still imagine I'm in that room again. I watch the girl I love, a silhouette waiting upon what I haven't thought to give. Outside, revelers stumble, laugh. The floral scent of gin drifts into the apartment; a drunk's baritone swells, then falls silent.

Julian aside, she put a halt to spending time with old friends. Each morning, she went to the college pool, looping back and forth in fast, obsessive laps. Phoebe's ass tightened. Thighs expanded. Unexpected muscles jutted against pale skin: a new Phoebe, fresh-hewn, more powerful than the original. In direct light, her head looked as if she'd tinted it sea-witch green. It brought to mind the bronze statues on the central lawn, stone-eyed heroes oxidized to verdigris.

She also kept going to John Leal's house, meeting with his group. Jejah, he called it, in tribute to the new life he'd started since the gulag. They talked, ate, rolled out the piano. Explored Bible passages. I asked if that meant anything, Jejah. If it translated.

It means "disciple," in Korean, she said.

Oh, I said. I'd changed my approach. I joked; I asked occasional questions, but I tried to hide what I felt. I still hoped this experiment, Phoebe's flirtation with belief, might lose its appeal. I'll admit I found Phoebe's notion of faith childish. It was a whim, I thought, a foolish hope she hinged on His alleged promises, the old, beguiling lies. He'd lift us up, rescind all death. In short, she wished to love the Lord because.

But I loved Phoebe, period. I had no rationale behind prizing, for instance, Phoebe's pointed chin. The full-blown mouth. I treasured for its own sake Phoebe's tongue sliding between my lips, its salt taste the daily host. Minute dots flecked ticklish legs. I'd licked the spots; I traced snail-lines while she shivered, laughing. Enough, she said. But I persisted. I baptized private constellations. If I hadn't counted the individual hairs, I'd still claimed each inch of Phoebe's skin. She wasn't even a Christian, she told me, one night, as we walked to Gibb Hall for a Phi Epsilon's choral recital. Wind blew silk around Phoebe's thighs. She'd been reading the Davenport translation of sayings attributed to Christ. Though she found His ideas compelling, she wasn't at all sure she believed in God. I'd like to, she said. It isn't enough. Well, you know how it is.

I'd saved enough in Beijing that I could plan a short trip. Driving us north in Phoebe's coupe, I kept the destination, Cape Cod, a surprise. It's Maine, she said.

No.

Ohio.

I shook my head. Phoebe's guesses leaped east, south, flouting logic. Istanbul, she tried. Delhi. Beirut. I said yes to Nairobi, yes to Taipei. If I had the cash, I thought, but I would. In time, if she'd wait, I'd be able to take us where she liked. We'd watch the lights of alien cities rush beneath the plane, strewn pearls we'd reach down to grab.

I drove until the beach house, a clapboard one-bedroom with a potbellied stove. I carried in the bags. I tore newsprint, then I crumpled it into long ropes. I snapped kindling. Bundled logs had been left at the stove's burned mouth. In minutes, I had the fire going. Wine bottles clanged as Phoebe lined them along the wall. I pan-fried trout; we split a cold Friuli. Pants rolled, we walked across the beach. The sea hissed, stinging exposed skin. It sucked the wet earth from beneath our feet. The next morning, we had Bellinis with toast, then we lolled on the sun porch, reading from old, salt-bloated magazines. Light spilled through closed eyelids, and I was turning into gold.

On Sunday, I drove us back to Noxhurst through light rain, leaving when we finished lunch. Phoebe, it turned out, had a Jejah meeting at five. She put a bare foot up on the dashboard, touching it to the windshield. Small haloes of body heat materialized around each unpainted toe. She switched on the radio, singing along. I didn't recognize the tune. She fell quiet. I turned down the music to let Phoebe doze.

Hours passed, then she lifted her head. Hello, she said. I might have had too much wine at lunch. Poor Will, I left you alone. What time is it? She glanced around, blinking. So much traffic.

It was fine until a minute ago, I said, as the radio clock flickered to 4:11. It should let up.

But how long will it take before we get to Noxhurst?

If this traffic doesn't stop, we're about an hour's drive from town.

Will, she said, voice high. I have to be at the meeting by five.

No, that's *if* the traffic doesn't improve. There's nothing to worry about, since it won't happen.

Phoebe strained in the seat, trying to look above the cars ahead of us. I wasn't sure why I'd said what I had. She'd be on time, as I knew well enough.

Maybe we should take local streets, she said.

Why are you so upset? I'll get you there.

I can't be late.

I told you I'd get you there.

In the expanding silence, Phoebe pulled up her legs. She turned aside, but I still heard the panic thrum. I cracked the window open. I drove. The traffic had slowed to a standstill. I bullied hesitating cars. I shoved into each hint of a rift. I pushed; I lunged, while Phoebe's left foot jigged. The key to driving fast in traffic is to act as if everyone else has more to lose. I willed

Phoebe to complain. I wanted the fight, but since she kept quiet, I couldn't start arguing without also being in the wrong.

Before long, traffic opened out. The wheels rushed across wet asphalt, a sound like film reel unwinding. The trip rolled back, as though it hadn't happened. In a short while, we'd hurtled past the speed limit.

Do you want to know why I have to be on time?

Sure, I said, but she fell silent again, a hand lighting on my thigh, until I turned off the highway, into Noxhurst. Since school reopened, she said, Jejah had begun holding group confessions. Each person talked about his life, and hers, inviting questions, criticism. It was optional. If she wasn't explaining this well, it was because she hadn't taken a turn, not yet. She would, tonight. It was on the schedule. I might have noticed she'd been writing, at times—well, that was what she'd been doing. Drafting thoughts. It would be rude to be late. I parked in front of the house, and I asked what she hoped to tell them.

I'll talk about my mother, she said. If I can. I don't think I've told you how she died, the details. That night, I insisted on driving, but I wasn't good at it. I hadn't practiced enough. She didn't like me to drive. In the last mile, going home, I was blinded by headlights. I swerved, then I hit a truck head-on. But she pitched her body in front of mine, taking the impact. I didn't even have to go to the hospital. Will, I think you were right. It could help, talking about it.

The door chimed open. I felt the light brush of a kiss, soft lips sliding, and then she left. I watched as she walked up the path, the front door swinging wide to let her in.

———

But this wasn't the kind of help I'd had in mind. I drove home, thinking of all the nights I woke to find Phoebe thrashing, caught in the sheets. I called her name until she sat up; I kissed Phoebe's fists, the knuckles tipped bone-white. What's wrong, I asked, afraid, knowing who she'd seen again, the ghost who dug herself out from an L.A. grave. She rang the doorbell, half-rotted, but alive. Finding Phoebe in the pool, she said, Hold my head beneath the surface until I drown. They stood on a rooftop, and she advised Phoebe to give her a push. I can't do it alone, Haejin, she said. It has to be you.

Each time, I rubbed Phoebe's rigid back. I'm here, I said. She fell asleep, wet hands balled at her head. Without fail, the next morning, she declined to talk about what she'd revealed. I think you should talk to someone, I said. But I talk so much, she said, flashing a smile. I'm talking to you. Someone who's qualified, I said. Maybe, ah, a therapist. I thought of my own mother's trouble: she'd admitted herself into the hospital this past June, while I was living in Beijing. She hadn't told me until she signed out. It's just that I wanted a break, she'd said. I didn't want you fretting, she added, as if, knowing what she'd hidden, I wouldn't fret more than I had.

But I'm an immigrant, Phoebe said. Immigrants don't believe in therapists. The Koreans I've known would judge it to be a failure of will, the kind of thing that happens to other ethnicities: it's like being lazy, or unfilial. I think a therapist could help you, I said. If I'm going to be honest, she said, I don't see the point. For me, that is. I understand people find it useful, but, okay, let's assume I wish my mother hadn't died. It's not worth examining. Julian says the most dispiriting words in the English language are "Red or white?" but, obviously, he's wrong. What's worse is "Last night, I dreamed," and—

She riffed like this until I stopped. If I tried again, insisting she find help, Phoebe's smile widened. It lit the girl up. In a glade of light, she slipped away. It was an act; I knew that, but I suppose I let it happen. Even now, I'll admit, if I recall these night fits, part of me wants to protest that this wasn't Phoebe: that the girl I loved, for instance, during a childhood trip to Delphi, went jumping through its ruins. Since she hadn't told me much else about it, I'd filled in the details until I might have been there, too, our earliest lives conjoined. On the crowded bus ride from Athens to Delphi, this Phoebe slept against my arm. The guide lectured into a microphone. It's the omphalos, he said. The holiest site, navel of the Hellenic world. In time, the bus rolled to a halt. Phoebe stood in the white, hot wash of sun; she rubbed light-blind eyes. Despite the heat, I held Phoebe's hand. I kept it in mine while we leaped the ancient stones, raising exuberant brumes of dust.

———

The day after the Cape Cod trip, as we left the apartment, I asked if I could attend the next Jejah meeting. Right, Phoebe said, with a laugh. I explained I wasn't kidding. Pulling on a white pashmina, she looked at me through its soft folds. It was raining again. I held the umbrella for both of us. We walked to Latham Hall while I told Phoebe partial truths. I've noticed the effect it's had on you, I said. You've spent so much time with this group. I want to know more about it. Since it's important to you, I can't help being curious.

She kept her face tucked down, hidden in the cashmere pile, until, lifting her head, she said she'd give John Leal a call. We'd arrived at the Latham gate. She hesitated, phone in hand. I left Phoebe the umbrella, and I said I'd walk ahead.

I waited in front of the dining hall, shielded from rain by the stone arcade. Croquet wickets littered the ground. That morning, I'd passed a group of old men in pastels and wan hats, batting mallets: alumni, I figured. But in the fog they'd been wraiths, sprung from time. Balls tocked, skinkling, through delicate arches. My head pulsed. I'd had too much to drink the previous evening. She was still on the phone. I watched as she talked. Hanging up, she came to tell me he'd apologized, but it wasn't possible. The group just didn't have the space. Not yet, at least.

I kept asking questions; I'd knock until they'd let me in. This has been the cardinal fiction of my life, its ruling principle: if I work hard enough, I'll get what I want. He heard God's voice, she said. He'd told the group the miracle could happen for each of them, if they practiced. If they had discipline. He believed in physical training. Once, he'd had Jejah dig a large hole in the backyard. They'd labored for hours with the hard-packed dirt, after which he had them fill it in again. But a little pain cleared the mind, he said. It made space for the waiting Spirit.

Then, as I walked to class one afternoon, I saw him, the soiled hems of his jeans trailing naked feet. His torso riding his hips like a serpent on its coil. From his gait alone, a lax, rolling, low-hipped stroll, I could have picked him out from a crowd. I stayed well behind him; I didn't think he'd spotted me, but it wasn't long after this that I had my chance. In bed, while I studied, Phoebe told me that the blond girl in Jejah, Tess, had quit. If you still want to come to a meeting, you're invited, she said.

I'll be there, I said.

It isn't a joke, though, she said. Don't come if all you'll do is laugh at it—

I won't laugh, I said.

I'm serious, Will.

So am I.

I twisted my face into a scowl, mock-solemn; she pushed me. Unbalanced, she tumbled on top of me. We rolled to the edge of the bed, and almost fell. Will, careful, she said, but she was laughing. She butted against my chest.

Don't laugh, I said. This is serious.

I kissed Phoebe's head, the strands gliding between my lips. I tasted chlorine. Irritated, I stopped. It was too hot, I realized. I opened a window, letting the light cold drift in. Phoebe caught ash-white flakes, ice shreds, on her fingertips. She blew them at me, but they'd melted. We were talking, until we weren't. She felt beneath my boxers; I pulled down ribbed tights, the bared thighs white. I listened to Phoebe's quick breaths. I shut my eyes, then a line of imagined girls pirouetted through: twirling, pouting figurines. To my surprise, not one looked like Phoebe, and the last thought before I finished was that I'd broken free of my girlfriend for several minutes. Like the breeze, this change came as a relief.

20.

JOHN LEAL

He loved to think of heaven, he said. Think of the psalmist's plea, his love song: whither shall I escape from Thy Spirit? he'd asked, knowing there's no escaping Him. While they lived on earth, they might still hide beneath the flesh. But dying, they'd be given up naked to the light. That's all death is, he said. It's an unveiling. In time, they'd show like flares.

21.

PHOEBE

I did plan to go to Beijing, Phoebe told Jejah. She flushed, then went pale again. While she talked, I might have been home, waiting. Maybe I was in the middle of a Michelangelo's shift, clearing basil-flecked plates. I fold napkins, and I align them in white triangles. The shining knives lie flat. She pulls her ponytail, the tip soft, wide, like a paintbrush. I'm awash with images. If I'd been with Phoebe on this night—and sometimes I see it all in such bold detail I think I was—I'd have said it's fine, I'm here, forget Beijing.

You should have seen Will when he learned he won his internship, she said. He flailed across the suite to me, half-naked, fists raised. Flinging himself on the futon, he settled his head on my thigh. Come with me, he said. Let's go to China. He reached up to grab my face, and he pulled it down to his. But I didn't need convincing. I said yes, I'll go. He shouted, jubilant. I'll go with you, I kept saying, just so that I could listen to him shout again.

For a while, I pitched myself into learning about Beijing. It was going to be my first real trip to Asia. Though born in Seoul, I'd left when I was still so little I kept nothing of it. So, I explored travel guides. I compiled best-of lists: Tanzhe Si. Houhai. I plotted which sections of the Wall we'd hike, picked restaurants. Online, at night, I studied photos of temples and red-tiled palaces. Tourists' frilled parasols, like stiff blooms, roved the imperial pavilions.

I told Will what I learned. Listen to this, I said. Palace eunuchs relied on chili paste for a local anesthetic, nothing else. They rubbed it on, then, chop. Half the aspiring eunuchs died, but, hey, if they survived, they'd get rich. They all belonged to peasant families. One cut, then a palatial life. No men but eunuchs lived on imperial grounds. Even the emperor's sons had to be banished from court the minute they learned to crawl. Oh, plus, eunuchs kept the genitals pickled. In jars. They hoped to be reunited in the afterlife.

Will laughed, as I'd known he would. But then, Noxhurst opened with spring, the trees bud-tipped, and I started losing interest in the trip. It wasn't his fault. I'd been wasteful. It's as if, or so I've, at times, believed, a pleasure has its allotted limit, a finite portion of juice in each pistil. I'd sucked it all out, anticipating.

If I went with him, Will would have his job, while I'd, what, visit old palaces? I'd take banal pictures. Jostle along with the hordes—a tourist, like them. One night, I admitted to Will that I didn't know what I'd do while he was working.

Do anything, he said. He didn't look up from his book. I tapped his wrist, impatient, until he put the book down. Take a class, if you want. In, ah, the fine art of Sichuan cuisine.

I flinched; noticing, he said, fast, No, it's what I'd do if I, I love Sichuan food. Phoebe, forget it. I'm joking! Just come. If you don't go, I won't. It was fine. I let it pass, though I heard what he'd implied, the insult left unsaid, that he'd enroll in a cooking class if he didn't have his own, real pursuits. Well, he had a point. I saw them spin, like tops: a lifetime's stack of plates I hadn't been allowed to wash, whirligig red-gold globes of fruit I hadn't peeled. I still couldn't cut an apple without nicking myself. When I tried, knives slipped. Dishes fell, goblin-bewitched. The logic behind this upbringing: if I didn't learn how to be in a kitchen, no one could keep me there. It wasn't a spell. It was a gift, one I had put to no use at all.

———

In the spring, I learned my grades might prohibit going to Beijing with Will. I let it be what happened; I failed. I'll miss you, I said. I kissed his hairline. He turned away, his forehead pinched, high. I didn't like causing him pain, but I couldn't have tagged along. I kissed him, again. I didn't stop until he turned back to me, still so trustful: like a child, finding solace with the person who'd hurt him in the first place. I took Will to his flight, then I returned, alone, to Noxhurst. The suite locked shut. Its silence rang like an alarm. I sat on the futon, at a loss. I didn't have a friend in town.

The June hours swelled, humid, dull, waiting to be filled. At parties, listless bodies held iced drinks to hot, moist skin. The college had no air-conditioning, and I kept thinking I should get a window unit. If I bought it, though, I'd be obliged to haul it home. I'd have to install it. I thought of the time a pigeon had flown into my suite, how it had crashed, flapped, rattling around, the trapped bird too panicked to find an exit. It dotted the living room white with shit. I was shrieking; Julian, too. Liesl ran to the landing, but Will stayed calm. He caught the pigeon with an upended trashcan. Sliding a flattened shoebox beneath the plastic lip, he carried it out. If Will were here, he'd have long since solved the air-conditioning problem. Instead, I sprawled on damp sheets. I listened to flash storms, too hot to sleep. Will's fund in Beijing required most of his time; often, he couldn't talk.

Julian was living in Manhattan. I could have gone to him, except that, like Will, he'd objected to the plan of staying in Noxhurst. I predict anguish, he'd said. Phoebe, you're a capable girl, but I'm afraid being alone isn't a skill. It's a disposition. I didn't want to prove him right; still, one night, I had to call him.

Julian, help, I said. In minutes, I'd packed a small bag, hopped in a taxi, and claimed an aisle seat in the air-conditioned train to New York. With a short walk, I exited the station. I hailed a second cab, which sped downtown. It dropped me in front of his building. Up the last flight of stairs, then I fell in Julian's arms. Give me that bag, he said. I've made big plans.

He didn't say, I told you so. We walked to a bistro, and piled into a red banquette. Julian's friends traipsed in, including his boyfriend. Hahn's a poet, Julian had explained. He bartends on the side. Phoebe, I'm afraid to jinx it, but—I haven't felt like this in so long. I made sure to sit next to Hahn. He kept quiet, so I asked questions; I joked, I teased, until I had him laughing. Since Julian loved this Hahn, I would, too.

Bills paid, we rode taxis to a karaoke place, then crowded into a private room. I have bonbons, Julian said. He distributed round pills, blithe with the pleasure of giving. I flicked a switch, to see what would happen. Disco-ball lights, jewel ovals, slid along the walls. Hahn and I duetted, hitting each note. I high-fived him, and I downed soju. People sang, while I kicked up a dance. Time flared. I sat with Hahn again, his arm tight at my waist. I leaned into the hold, liking his strength, then I felt his hand shift, warm, inside the shirt. He'd slipped, I thought. But his hand pushed up. He gripped breast flesh, and pinched it. Everyone was singing.

I stood; I went to Julian, who hadn't noticed. He touched his lips to the side of my head. I should tell him, I thought. But in that small box of a private room, I'd insisted on dancing. No one had joined me as I performed. Will often recalled the night I'd met him, how I'd looked, hands raised. Phoebe, I could have watched all night, he said. It's just that I love to dance, I said, with a shrug. I'd known full well what I was doing, though. I'd felt his attention pull taut, alert, like a long puppet string. I tugged it; his eyes moved, helpless. In the spotlight I'd compelled, Will's wide-eyed stare, I came back to life. I hadn't tried to flirt with Hahn, but I had. He'd believed I wanted him to touch me; then, when he put his hand into my shirt, I hadn't protested. Instead, I'd let Julian's boyfriend admire me.

This is what I do, I thought. It's who I am. I hurt those I love. In the morning, I left a note on Julian's table. I woke up feeling unwell, it said. I took the first train back to school.

22.

WILL

I half-ran through Platt courtyard, taking the diagonal path. On the frozen lawn, a small group huddled around a picnic table, cigarette tips burning. I rushed past while someone slung a girl across his back. Help, she wailed. I paused, uncertain. Put me down, you big dolt, she said, but then she let out a howl that rolled into a laugh. I kept going. I made it to the Hilcox gate with less than a minute left. I'd switched a night shift to be here. I opened my coat to let in the cold. It was several minutes past the assigned time, then six. Fifteen. Don't be late, he'd said. White disembodied masks floated toward me, cloaks rustling.

Close those eyes, Will.

I was blindfolded, wrists tied behind my back. Instructed to walk, I took a few steps, hesitant. I was pushed, lifted into a tight space. I touched rough, short-piled fabric, then a metal ridge: I'd been put in a car trunk. The chilled glass of a bottle nudged my palm.

Drink this.

I forced down a harsh liquid, and then I was told to tuck my head in. The lid banged shut. The engine surged, then settled. Tasting bile, I held it back. I'd attended Jejah meetings a month before John Leal said I could be initiated. In all this time, I'd taken part in nothing more alarming than long-winded Bible studies. I hadn't heard a single confession. No one dug holes, and even John Leal's talk of hearing God sounded like orthodox delusion, the usual born-again cant. But if Jejah evinced signs of being less fanatical than I'd thought, I wasn't relieved. I intended to be let in. If I could learn what, exactly, had attracted Phoebe, which conjuring tricks he'd used, I'd be able to prove his show wasn't real. Watch his hand, I'd explain. That flick of a wrist. I'd practiced His illusions, as well; expert, I could pull Phoebe free.

The car stopped, and then the trunk opened. I had trouble staying upright. I swayed, blind, while invisible hands impelled me forward. I felt a rush of warmth: we'd gone inside. Sounds echoed; voices, chanting. I listened to find Phoebe, but I couldn't. Still clothed, I was led into a lukewarm pool. I was told to take a deep breath, and strong hands pushed my shoulders down. I plunged in. The blindfold slipped. I saw the light-spangled tiles, John Leal's blue-veined feet. It was peaceful, the water like soft glass. When he let go, I almost wished he hadn't.

I knew, of course, the substance of what Phoebe longed to find. The loss restituted, a vital hurt made whole. But I'd been a kid when I tried to attain the same result; then, because I had to, I'd grown up. John Leal tapped my head. I surfaced, listing close to him. I caught my reflection in his pupils, but he fixed the blindfold back in place.

It didn't seem like much of an initiation: a routine alcoholic hazing, I thought, at first. It wasn't unlike what I'd done to join Phi Epsilon. Even the baptism had its parallel. In Gibb fountain, along with the other pledges, I'd stripped down to bright pink fishnet tights. I hula-hooped while shouting the college anthem in pig Latin.

In hindsight, though, the Jejah initiation draws a dividing line. The meetings lengthened; activities changed. With John Leal's urging, we whirled in circles until we fell. To spin us out of the head, he said, and into a waiting Lord. He assigned tasks to stipulated hours, psalm-based chants we had to recite. While my time with Jejah predated John Leal's best-known penalties, I did spend a long evening in the Litton Street backyard digging a hole, then filling it back in. Since I was the newest initiate, I had the most to do. I was prideful, he said. I required breaking down. In the morning, I ran a prescribed five miles along the Hudson.

I'd have liked to swim with Phoebe instead, but he kept the tasks separate.

I followed his assignments, even in private. I intended, I thought, to avoid being ·found out. Since I was inauthentic, a fraud, I had to put on a good act to prove otherwise. With Phoebe, too, I hid what I was thinking. It wasn't all lies, though. In giving my first confession, for instance, I tried to be truthful. I was asked to confront my failings: to cultivate openness before Jejah, he said, so before God. Sitting in the middle of the circle, I told them I hadn't wanted to lose my faith. I'd proselytized to anyone who'd listen. I went house to house, selling Christ: a fanatic, and proud of it. I told them about the Beijing mission trip, then the shock of my father's betrayal. I'd tried to help the parent I still had, but it wasn't enough. I wasn't enough. I'd knelt in the bedroom, asking one last time for a sign. Thin curtains fluttered, gauze-white, and I waited until I couldn't, then I got up. It became hard to live at home. The walls were thin. In bed, I heard my mother's frenzied petitions to God, asking Him to heal me. I thought of my father's lot, atheist in a household bent on bringing him to Christ. It didn't excuse what he'd done, but I could touch the edges of his solitude. Like him, I fled. I came here. I realized I had to lie—

Oh, had to lie, John Leal said, impatient.

I believed I had to lie, I said. I felt as if I didn't exist. Nietzsche says shame is inventive, but—

I don't care what Nietzsche said. Will, I don't want you to try to impress us, parading borrowed quotations—don't tell us why, after having read Nietzsche, you think lying happens. Tell us why *you* lied.

I was ashamed, I said. I wanted a new life, so I invented it. It helped, too. I wish I hadn't lied to you, Phoebe, but with anyone else, if the option came up, I'd do it again.

I paused until I saw him nod. Keep going, he said. I didn't look at Phoebe, though I felt she was listening. I pointed everything I said in the single direction of my girlfriend, sitting with the others. This went on, lasting hours at a time. I kept explaining, while they'd interrupt. They'd ask questions, pushing me to tell more than I intended—in principle, they. Most often, though, it was him. Nights ended with John Leal pacing the hearth, agitated, his odd, zigzag gait picking up speed as he preached. He told us that, while still enrolled at Edwards, he'd founded a Christian group that pulled in hundreds of students; he implied he'd led large-scale rallies, charismatic revivals. Since the gulag, he'd lost interest in big crowds. Instead, the Lord had called him, His apostle, to this more private kind of service. Here, he said, like this. With us.

But I could picture his stage act. He'd have flaunted how close he felt to the Lord. It was, I realized, one of his principal tricks. I want to tell you about God, he said, then did. He performed his religion, discalced, talking to Christ. Mid-sentence, he broke into ecstatic song. Filled with the Spirit, he said. Tall firelight lapped at the ceiling while he signaled to each of us in turn; he shouted, flinging up his arms. Most would-be Christians, he said, insist too much on faith. But all God looks to find in us is desire. If we want Him, belief spills in. It rises to His level, and it will fill the void. Isn't that right, Lord. Real faith isn't about laws, moral prohibitions. No, Lord. He cited early Christians, the saints who'd received His visions. Like them, he heard God's voice. He'd seen His face, and lived. But all this could be made available to us, if we tried.

———

Even before she joined Jejah, I valued what clues I could find. I'd studied, for instance, the handful of old novels she'd brought from L.A. Soft with use, they proved Phoebe's claim that she used to love reading. She'd underlined words, filled margins, the penciled notes fading. I asked why she'd stopped; I lost interest in it, she said. I'd examined the glyphs as I might have a coded map, directions to Phoebe's shining, inmost psyche, that visible opacity, which showed itself in allowing me to sight it hiding. Privation is lust; isolation, desire. I craved what she withheld. I always wanted to know more about how it felt, being Phoebe.

Then, Phoebe took up Jejah, and I sat in the circle while she divulged secrets: more, often, than she'd let slip with me. He raised questions; obedient, she replied. I tried to believe she was also talking in my direction, but it was obvious she wasn't. If,

alone, on the way home from a meeting, I alluded to what she'd
said, she'd give me a quick kiss, a laugh. No, let's talk about you,
she said. I haven't had a minute with you all night. Tell me about
the lunch shift. Did you find out who hid the pipe in the trash?

In the Seoul before you and I lived, John Leal told us, a unified
land, everyone learned the same songs. It wasn't unusual, he
said, in this city of Phoebe's birth, to have one person begin
singing a ballad in public. Others would join in. He loved to
picture it, the heads lifting to sing in chorus. If this Seoul hadn't
existed, he still wanted to think it had. Korea dispatched more
Christian apostles abroad than any nation but the U.S. Per cap-
ita, it placed first. It could well take the lead. The next fount of
revival, he called it. No one was more spiritual than Koreans
could be; no believers, more devoted. It was a land of purists. He
talked about present-day Seoul, where lit-up, blinking signs jutted out like flags on a pole. You'll have to see it, he said.

I'm not sure when I began to suspect the act had turned real, that
I was staying in Jejah as much to help myself as Phoebe. If I was
going to put this time into the group, I thought, I might as well
give it a chance. It felt like the last attempt. Often, I thought of

an afternoon I'd spent evangelizing in San Francisco. In the evening, before driving home to Carmenita, I met with my cohort of Jubilee students to hold closing prayers on Fisherman's Wharf. Docked boats shone in fading light. We raised linked hands, calling out in tongues. People with no experience of God tend to think that leaving the faith would be a liberation, a flight from guilt, rules, but what I couldn't forget was the joy I'd known, loving Him. Thou hast turned for me my mourning into dancing—the old, lost hope revived. I was tantalized with what John Leal said was possible: I wished him to be right.

She'd always been more Julian's friend than Phoebe's, and it was Julian who called with the news. There wasn't a final note, no sign of intent. No one could tell if she'd slipped on the Midwest ice, if it was an accident, but Liesl had fallen from a third-story attic windowsill of the St. Paul house. It wasn't a long fall. She should have survived; instead, she cracked her head open on a fence post. Within hours of arriving at the hospital, she'd died.

Edwards students flew to St. Paul for the funeral, Phoebe included. I said I'd go along. Don't, she said. She spent the night in a hotel, with Julian. He then decided he'd stay an extra night in St. Paul, so I picked Phoebe up from the airport. She looked exhausted, ponytail unwashed. I have a fresh pot of lentil chili, I said. I've ordered laziji, too. It should be here in minutes.

She tried to smile. I don't have much of an appetite, she said. Maybe in the morning.

I asked what I could do. I'll be fine, she said. She went to bed. It's not that I believed Phoebe, but I did think that, if she wanted to be alone, I shouldn't intrude. She and Liesl, I'll repeat, hadn't been at all close. But during the next Jejah meeting, I glanced up to see Phoebe talking quietly to John Leal, crying. She pushed a hand to her open mouth, almost covering it. He took hold of Phoebe's chin: he tilted it until she was forced to look at him.

———

She started talking about hoping to visit Seoul. I should be able to picture it, she said. But I left when I was an infant, and I haven't visited it once. People tell me I'm the whitest Asian girl they've met. I think they figure it's a compliment. I've heard it as one. Will, I used to take pride in knowing so little about what I'm from. John Leal calls it self-hatred, and it is. He's right. I don't want to be this kind of a person.

I nodded, though I had trivial points I might have raised. Small cavils I left unvoiced. The fact that she'd hop on a plane to go to Seoul, but not to visit me, in Beijing, as she'd promised: that was one. I also could have brought up, but didn't, the fact that he wasn't even Korean.

His mother, she'd object. She——

He's half.

Well, yes. But still.

The more I heard of Phoebe's confessions, the less certain I felt as to how I should respond. Exhibit 1.1: the lineup of men. I hadn't known. They'd predated me, she said, but I couldn't help seeing the oil of all the hands, like starfish prints, staining Phoebe's skin. I trusted Phoebe, I did; I also noticed, though, that she looked at him as if at a riddle she had to solve. I told myself I was mistaken. I'd had a newlywed friend at Jubilee, Ivan, whose wife had trouble being faithful. His wits love-honed, he learned to predict who she'd pick next. She had a specific type, he explained. Baseball-capped toughs with stiff posture, the kind of shits who start parking-lot fights. Before long, he could tell before she did. It was what ended the relationship: he accused his wife of sleeping with a best friend's husband. But she hadn't, not yet. He refused to believe the denial, until, giving in, she turned to what he'd pointed out.

John Leal told us we'd have to attend a protest in Manhattan, a pro-life march. It's taking place this Saturday morning, he said. I know it's not much notice, but Christ is asking us to be with

Him. John Leal outlined a plan he'd established with local churches, to drive to New York with people, supplies, and then he swept into one of his wild soliloquies, telling us again about the time he'd helped a desperate girl in the gulag abort a half-foreign child. Though he saved the girl's life, he still wept if he thought about the fetus he pulled out, its recognizable fist.

It was close to midnight when I walked home with Phoebe. She'd lent the car to Julian. He was in New Haven, visiting old boarding-school friends. The night was mild. I'd fallen behind with studying, and I was tired. I hadn't slept; I wished to be home. I'd have proposed calling a taxi, but, the previous evening, I'd discovered I didn't have my half of the month's rent. I was still working a partial load at Michelangelo's, a few night shifts each week. Ling had offered me a follow-up research position, a role extending the last project; I turned it down, since I had no time. I referred him to a fellow Phi Epsilon. Short of options, I had to activate a credit card I'd once received, unsolicited, in the mail. I didn't want the debt. I'd learned what harm a credit habit might inflict. I'd kept the card just in case, for emergencies, positive I wouldn't use it. But then, last night, I'd pulled a label off the plastic, the adhesive giving up its hold with sickening ease: like mother, like son.

What's more, if I went to the march, I'd have to switch Saturday's shift for a less profitable slot. More cash lost. The trip would involve spending, too. I wanted to quiz Phoebe as to what she thought of it. By the time I joined Jejah, they'd stopped picketing

Phipps clinic; why, she hadn't known. She'd never protested the clinic, she'd said, but she believed, as I did, that abortions should remain legal. I didn't think she could have changed her mind. We waited at the light. Instead, while a flesh-pink neon sign, Tivoli, fizzed behind us, I asked about the first gulag story he'd told. The pregnant girl, I said. Lina. Mina. She was kicked in the stomach. You told me about it: she died, then trailed him. Is this one girl?

I saw a taxi turning, its sign lit. No, they couldn't be, Phoebe said, at last.

I flagged down the cab. In silence, we rode home. I've examined this night, Phoebe. I've rethought what I said to you, and I'm still sure of this much: I kept quiet a long time, then I asked a single question.

23

JOHN LEAL

He wasn't just his Lord's child: he often had to be His substitute. Proxied liaison, latest in the line of soloist prophets. In His service, there wasn't a single opening he wouldn't exploit. No gambit existed that he'd have fancied beneath him; he would give, if it helped, anything. The Lord had peeled the flesh off His corpse. He had spread it as a bloodied veil upon this earth, a flailed red carpet to ease His people's fall. Others might ask how long, but he could wait. Faith is a long patience. Minutes tremble, he told his group, with the hope of revelation. Each particle of dust breathes forth its rejoicing. The stripped Noxhurst trees spelled out the Lord's writing, if they'd learn to see it. God is, not was. He, John Leal, had called them as heroes. The Lord had laid His hand upon their heads.

24.

PHOEBE

The night I came back to Noxhurst from Julian's, Phoebe said, I tried calling Will. He was still in his office, in Beijing. The call wasn't scheduled, but he picked up. He asked what was wrong. Nothing, I said, and he hesitated. He thought I sounded upset. Well, it's hot, I said. Maybe that's what you're hearing. If you're sure, he said. I told him I was, but I came home the next afternoon to find boxed peonies in the hall, a gift from Will. The lush, open-lipped petals, flaring signal-red, indicated he thought I'd lied. I left the bouquet in place. Outside, the light was harsh, startling. A high-bodied bus listed past, piping exhaust. I imagined going right, angling into its path. But I wasn't going to walk into traffic; foolish, then, to pretend otherwise.

———

I still had peonies spoiling in the hall the June morning I opened a one-line email from John Leal, inviting me to his house again. Since the first time, I'd declined his invitations. Instead, to be polite, I'd had a drink with him, the occasional lunch. I'm not religious, I told him. I know that, he said. I'm just hoping to be friends. This time, though, I felt alone. I said yes. It wasn't until I attended the third house meeting that I asked what had inspired him to persist so long. The first language of God is silence, he said. You'll have to sweep the temple steps awhile before He'll call to you. But He will. Phoebe, believe it or not, God tells me you'll be essential to His plan. It's the truth. In His name, yours will be magnified.

———

No, I didn't believe in God's plan. Still, I liked listening to him talk. It had so little to do with the life I'd known. I kept thinking I'd go to one last meeting, then quit. I went again. He noticed I fidgeted, and he advised I exercise, as they did. It'll be good for you, he said. He sounded playful, but when I laughed, he didn't. Unechoed, I heard an idiot, laughing at nothing. I stopped. He asked which kind of exercise I liked best. I told him I used to swim; he drew up a schedule. Before the piano, I'd loved being in the pool. I used to frolic with half-nereid L.A. friends: I showed off high flip dives, and I played Marco Polo until I lost my voice, but this wasn't fun. He set goals. I kept a log. One dull lap blurred into the next, tired leg muscles singing. Push through, he urged. Each night, I thrashed across the school's Olympic-sized pool. I watched myself, the blurred Phoebe ghost, glide along striped tiles. In time, I noticed more habits changing. I was drinking less, I realized. If I craved gin, I sipped tonic. I hadn't known it, but I longed for discipline. It was part of the life I'd lost with the piano: a schedule, rigid expectations. With the six-plus hours I practiced each night, I'd had rules to bind me in place. They'd held me up.

I started playing the piano again, in Jejah, at John Leal's request. I'd thought I couldn't, but in a short while, as with the ongoing swims, I didn't mind. Plinked single-octave hymns, simple chords that resolved, like finished stories, with each line: this wasn't the music I'd failed. If I played well, or didn't, I felt no pleasure. I didn't have to be afraid.

So, I'd changed. It was possible. I often thought about what John Leal liked saying, that if we could believe all people existed in their minds as much as we did in our own, the rest followed.

To love, he said, is but to imagine well. I pulled out this thought; I held it up, in private, turning it in the light as though I'd find in its prism gleam the Phoebe I could still become.

The next time my father called, I picked up, for once. I said hello. He asked how I was doing. We talked a bit. I tried imagining what he'd felt: this indulged first son, servant-coddled, chaebol hidalgo, used to getting what he wanted. Then, upheaval. Humiliation. Left behind in Seoul, trailing his wife and newborn child to L.A. He had to beg a month, alone in a hotel, before she'd let him live with us. His English was book-learned, ill-suited to fast-talking L.A. If he wished to buy cigarettes, the shop clerk asked him what he'd said. He had to point, like a child. The small Korean house church across town might have been a haven, the one place where he felt valued, whole. There, people knew who he was. His familial name inspired respect. He went again. Before long, he led services; he found an available lot, and helped build the house of God. He toiled. He hustled, until if, once in a while, he didn't uphold perfect self-control: if he flailed, and shouted, it hadn't been on purpose—was that it? I pained him with how fast I'd picked my mother's side, and did he hope, with his periodic calls, to retrieve lost time?

But then, late one night, as I was leaving the Litton Street house, John Leal let slip that he'd known I was rich. My mother's savings, the life insurance: it was a small fortune, which I'd obtained through killing the person I loved. I didn't go to the next Jejah meeting. I ignored John Leal's emails. He showed up at my suite, knocking until I let him in. I asked him to leave. I was shaking. It wasn't my father's right to tell you anything, I said. I haven't talked about it with a single friend, I didn't tell Will—

I know, he said. I do. Phoebe, listen. Maybe I shouldn't have brought it up. But, listen, your father talked to me about this a while ago. It was before I even realized I'd return to Noxhurst. He wasn't confiding in his daughter's friend. You and I hadn't met, and he just wanted advice. Phoebe, he was thinking about you, the guilt you've carried. He worried. I'm sure he still does.

It was August, the suite heat-swollen. I still hadn't put in an air-conditioning unit. I wiped my forehead, and he asked if I'd take a walk with him. It's cooled down, outside, he said. I didn't assent, but when he turned to leave, I followed him. He kept talking. What you've inherited is a gift, he said. No, it is. This doesn't mean you're obligated to keep it. You could pass it along. Phoebe, others are also in pain, and can use the help.

I'm not sure I could do that, I said.

Yes.

But I—

You can.

25.

WILL

We followed him as he pushed a path into the waiting crowd. The protest hadn't started yet, but wind rippled plastic-sheathed signs. Sunlit fetuses swung up, down, while flags flicked like striped tongues. John Leal halted; he spun, abrupt, and doubled back. I thought he'd tell us we'd taken a wrong turn. Instead, he butted his face up to mine, so close I felt his breath.

Will, he said. Oh, Will. He'd learned, he said, that I was full of questions. So, I was confused about his time in the gulag— which, all right, it had been a bewildering time for him, as well. Given I hadn't lived through it, how much more so for me. But why hadn't I brought my questions to him? It grieved him that I could still be this prideful. Think, he said, of John the Baptist telling us he couldn't touch the latchet of his Lord's shoes. I still hadn't learned how to be a disciple. It was high time I did. If, that is, I had it in me. I should kneel, he said.

He handed me a thin rag; he told me to wipe the others' shoes, then his feet. I cleaned each muddied shoe. Melted ice soaked cold into my jeans. I held his foot, working the rag through his toes. Flecks of tissue gleamed, like nacre, in the cracked skin. I was trying to think. His time in the gulag, he'd said. It was what I'd asked Phoebe. The question about Mina, but we'd been walking home. We'd left John Leal at his house. If he hadn't, how'd he—

I glanced at Phoebe, but she looked down. She'd turned red. Phoebe didn't blush often. If she did, the cause tended to be physical. She'd had too much alcohol, or it was hot. Phoebe hadn't been drinking, though. It was a cold morning. Each breath showed white. I wouldn't have believed it possible, but she still couldn't look at me. She'd gone to him with what I'd said.

It was past the time the march should have begun, and people were losing patience. I'll give it five minutes, then I'm calling it quits, a man said. Placards leaned against a building wall. I saw John Leal talking to people I didn't recognize. With a nod, he stepped on an upended crate. His mouth moved. In that hubbub, I couldn't pick out his words. Phoebe apologized again, tearful.

It's all right, I said, but she had more she wanted to explain. It's fine, I said. Hoping she'd calm down, I kissed Phoebe's head. I was intent on listening to John Leal's speech: I was curious what his effect would be with this large an audience, if they'd respond as we did. He lifted his head, pitching his voice.

. . . hands splashed with blood, he said. We're all here this Saturday morning, and I know I don't need to tell you the truth that an unborn child has a heartbeat before it's a month old. I don't have to tell you that, within the first three months of fetal life, a human infant's strong enough to grip a hand. But I'm not sure if it's done much good, all this truth. What point it's had, if you and I aren't saving lives.

Wind gusted, flapping nylon jackets. Instead of trying to talk across the noise, he held up his palm, indicating he'd wait. More people turned in his direction.

The Lord is calling us, he said. But we've failed, you and I, in following Him. We're living in a time of great evil. Rivers of blood, replenished with children's bodies, are flooding this nation, and we've let the blood spill. If we are lukewarm, the Lord has said, He will spit us out of His mouth. I'll ask you what I've asked myself, late at night, as I wait upon His Spirit: if the likes of you and I won't be radical for God, who will?

While he talked, his voice had risen. He finished with a shout, then he fell silent. The crowd around us was hushed, listening. Raising his head, he asked if he could get an amen. Several people replied; he asked again. This time, the amens belled toward him. I felt my ears ring. Yes, Lord, he said. Oh, Lord, I beg, be here with us. He called out the opening line of a hymn, one I recognized, and the crowd sang it back to him. Phoebe joined in, hands folded. She rocked back and forth, eyes closed, and I thought of the night we'd met, how she'd danced until she gasped for breath, holding the thick hair in a ponytail. It was damp at the tips. Sweat trickled down her slim throat. Phoebe's rolling hips parodied that night; so, too, the rapt, upheld face. She'd told me, as she apologized, that he'd asked how I was doing with Jejah. He'd spoken with love, she said, and she'd responded in kind, without thinking. I'm not upset with you, I said. I wasn't: she didn't have to apologize. I felt a long confusion lifting. If anything, I should be grateful. For some time, I'd also failed to think.

The crowd kept singing. I watched, alone. It was a horde, and they all had what I lacked. In what He's credited to have said, the Lord is explicit. He insists on full, absolute devotion, nothing less. John Leal had that part right. But from the start, I'd obeyed His call. I'd pledged my life to Him, if to no avail, which left me believing God had to be nothing, a fiction; that, or He didn't want me.

Fifteen minutes, a man said. The crowd shifted forward. I put a hand in my pocket, and I felt a twist of plastic wrap I'd forgotten bringing. It was a small bundle of prescribed sedatives, pills I'd grabbed at the last minute because Phoebe and I planned to stay in the city that night. I had enough trouble sleeping that I relied on these pills, the bottle's festive castanet rattle a promise, preludial to rest. Though I hadn't tried taking them except at night, before I went to bed, the pills also tranquilized. I could use a little extra calm, I thought. I opened the cellophane. To rush the effect, I chewed the pills.

———————

The march began. We'd been asked to walk in silence. Phoebe stayed close to me, a light hand at my back. The first time we showered in a shared stall, she'd pointed out the indent of my spine. This, she said. Here. She'd traced the rill, following the line down to my ass. I hadn't conceived, before then, of having a back worth noticing: now I did, the skin gilded with Phoebe's sight.

This situation, well, it was a crisis. The girl I loved was in a cult—and that's what it is, I thought, a cult. It was a problem, but I'd solve it, because I was intelligent. The sun's heat intensified. Disquiet thawed until, tranquil, awash, I almost sympathized with these people. If I were convinced that abortion killed, I, too, might think I had to stop the licit holocaust. It wasn't so long ago that I'd believed as they did. In fact, I pitied them. Goodwill toward all, I thought. While driving down from Noxhurst, I'd asked Phoebe, at last, if she agreed with the protest's object, having abortions outlawed. It isn't what I want to think, she'd said, but a fetus has a pulse within a month of fertilization. It's alive.

We marched awhile before the pill's effect changed shape. I'd been watching protest signs bob past, marveling at bloodied photos, when a fetus jumped down. Others followed, flailing. Infant fists lifted; placentas writhed like tails, trailing dots of blood. One fell inches from my foot. I squatted, and I picked it up to prevent its being trampled. It was small, not quite spanning my hand, so I retrieved a second twisting fetus, then a third. Phoebe crouched down with me. What's wrong? she whispered.

I asked if she'd give me the handbag; instead, she asked what I was doing. With my chin, I motioned toward my little charges, but I'd lost them. I looked around. White orthopedic shoes flitted past. She nudged me, repeating what she'd said. But they'd vanished. I'd imagined the field of fetal children. The first time I filled the sleeping-pill prescription, a pharmacist had cautioned me about potential side effects. Mild hallucinations, he'd said. This wasn't mild, though. I'd have to tell the pharmacist. Phoebe asked if I was hurt, so attentive it brought tears to my eyes. I'd taken a sedative, I explained. It was the pill I used to sleep, except, this time, I'd stayed awake. It had, perhaps, gotten a bit strong.

Stand up, she said, rising.

I tried; I couldn't. She helped me to my feet. The flesh of my arm bulged around Phoebe's tight grip. She released me, and kept marching. I focused on each step: left, then right. The next time I glanced up, John Leal was walking next to Phoebe. His hip grazed her side, so I tapped his arm. I have a question, I told him.

Not now, Will.

I—

We'll talk after this.

No, I said. This isn't a request. I want to talk.

His head tilted, as if to see me in a different light. He glinted at the edges, protean, slipping. I had to grab him while I still could. Pin him down until he'd admit to his shape-shifting lies. He rubbed his face. I can't help you, Will, he said. I've tried, but I don't have the time. To be honest, I've lost interest.

Before I could think of how I'd respond, Phoebe pulled me back. Soon, we'd left the protest behind. We stood out on the street, hailing taxis. Lines of cars sped past, cutting long scars in the slush. The cabs were all occupied. I'd forgotten where I'd parked. I watched the sidewalk flecks, blotted gum. The harsh dazzle of pitted ice. Wind stirred the trash. In a lost, past life, I'd fancied these to be coded messages, dispatches from a loving Lord. Each detail flashed with divine relevance, but it was a false hope. What I had instead was this: salted bitumen, an oil-stained plastic bag. I should give it more attention, not less. I swayed, trying to understand.

With a brush of kidskin, Phoebe put my hand to a lamppost. Hold this, she said. I'll be back in an instant. She crossed the plain of ice until I couldn't be sure which of the distant backs was hers. Folios of newsprint drifted. Close by, a girl in bright lipstick fiddled with a bike chain. She jumped on its seat; she lurched left, raincoat flaring out. The thin form grew a sail, a pale nephilim wing. I thought she'd fall, but she pinged the bike bell, then swept down the street.

Will, Phoebe called, leaning out from an idling cab. She took me to the station, waiting until the first train that would go north to Noxhurst. Once it pulled in, she talked the attendant into letting her on without a ticket. He doesn't feel well, and I'm not staying, she explained, giving him her smile.

Here, she said, pushing my seat into a recline. I tried to apologize, but she said she had to get back to the protest. She set my phone's alarm to ring before my stop.

What about the apartment? I asked, remembering. Your friend's place.

Oh, that, she said.

She took out her phone. I was about to say I could wait in the apartment until the protest finished, but she said, still looking at the phone, I'm staying the night. From the train, I watched Phoebe go, striding fast, horizontal. I'd have left the train, chased Phoebe down, if I'd been less to blame. The train slid into the afternoon, and I slept until the Noxhurst station.

———

Up through the next morning, in spite of what she'd said, I still thought Phoebe would come back Saturday night. But I woke Sunday to find she wasn't home. She also hadn't returned my calls. I should have studied; I opened a book, stared at it as long as I could, then poured a drink. I sat in the apartment through morning: I took a bus to Michelangelo's. Though I didn't have a shift, I helped at the front until I noticed a five-top littered with used plates. I carried them back to the kitchen, spilling pesto on my shirt. I dropped a knife. I took the table's busboy out back, and I yelled at him. I asked what the fuck he'd been thinking. Looking down, he muttered that it wasn't his table. It's Gil's, he said, his childish face bagged with fatigue. I excused him. I left, riding the bus home again.

The sun went down, and I called Phoebe. I left a short message asking if she'd let me know she was all right. Relying on the principle that almost nothing happens as I think it will, I started ticking through possible disasters. What I predicted, I'd forestall. I sat at the kitchen table. Each time I emptied a glass, I poured the next drink. It was 3:10 in the morning when the front door swung open. She stood in the hall, half-dissolved in porch light. Easing the lock into its slot, she set down a bag. She turned. Oh, she said, startled. It's you. What are you doing?

I closed the laptop, and, with it, all the light I'd had. I'd been searching traffic-accident reports. She flicked on the hall lamp. I saw Phoebe take in the gin bottle, the knit hat I still hadn't removed. Will, she said. I told you I was staying the night.

I didn't know when you'd be home. I kept calling.

My phone died, she said. I didn't notice it until a minute ago.

Hope rose, then fell. While she hung her coat and pashmina, I took a long, sustaining swig of tonic-splashed gin. The plaid skirt twitched on Phoebe's thighs, brass buttons gleaming. The phone had tolled through its full five rings before it prompted me to leave a message, which meant it had been on. If it hadn't, the phone would have shunted me to Phoebe's voicemail with just one ring. No, each time I called, the phone had vibrated. She'd pulled it out, seen *Will*, and put it back in the bag. I was able to see what she'd done, in such detail that I knew it had to be true. When I could, I asked how she'd gotten home.

I drove, she said. I, well, John Leal did. I was too tired. I'll make tea. Do you want anything?

Getting up, I went to the sink. I'll do it, she said, but she hesitated, then sat. I filled the kettle. From the cupboard, I took down the aged puerh I'd bought in Beijing's tea bazaar, a labyrinth I'd spent hours roving, intent on finding what she'd like best. It's the king of teas, the merchant had explained, pouring me a sample cup. Unable to decide, I'd tried so much tea I'd had to piss outside, behind the building. I broke off a piece. I crumbled it into the mesh basket. Puerh leaves unfurled, like relaxing fists.

You should have something, she said.

I don't want tea.

I'll bet you haven't eaten.

I hadn't, I realized. In a panic, I'd failed to eat since morning. She could tell, by looking at me, if I needed to eat. I took Phoebe the cup. She leaned into my side. With an arm swathed in cashmere, the soft fibers prickling, she pulled me close. My breathing slowed. Once, not long ago, she'd pointed to a picture on Julian's wall, a child with his arms flung out. Posed like a kite, she'd said. A kite, I repeated, the word unrolling a tableau of blanched sand. Heat. Light. Surfboards gliding, iridescent; swimmers beaded with sea foam. Harlequin kites spooled high, lolloping toward the sun. In that childhood photo, I couldn't avoid noticing a crucifixion pose, while she saw—a kite. I'd loved Phoebe's pagan mind, unpolluted with His blood. Phoebe, forgive me, I should have said, help me, but then she shifted to drink the puerh. Let go, I moved to sit at the table, a tall vase of white phlox dividing us. She inhaled steam. Wire hangers, I said.

What?

Bleach, I said. For millennia, women have tried to induce home abortions. They've drunk bleach, hot lye—even the Bible gives tips about this. Quinine. Hippocrates advises a prostitute to jump up and down. I told Phoebe about a high-school friend, Stu, who'd punched his knocked-up girlfriend in the stomach until she fainted. She asked to be kicked down the stairs. He'd done it, blinded with tears. The abortion she wanted was too expensive, and she had Baptist parents she couldn't tell. Once, a local wit, calling in to a radio show, was asked to explain what people did for fun in Carmenita, California. Get pregnant, he said. The kind of people she, Phoebe, knew would always be able to obtain abortions, while fifteen-year-old children in towns like mine spewed—*what?*

Phoebe shook, laughing. No, it's just, Will, you researched this. The quinine. You looked it up, getting all these points in line.

Tell me why you picked Christians, I said.

Excuse me?

You chose the one set of beliefs I wasn't going to be able to stand. I'm asking if it was on purpose, if it's something I did.

I can't fight tonight, she said. She pushed away the tea. It sloshed in the cup, without spilling. I'm so tired. I don't know what's happened, why you've turned against Jejah, but, please, let's go to bed. We'll argue in the morning, if you like.

I looked in the news, I said. From the spring before last, in Yanji, China. I searched headlines. John Leal's a U.S. citizen. If he'd been abducted by North Korean agents, his organization would have reported it. It would be a big fucking deal. "Edwards student missing, presumed kidnapped." But there's nothing, Phoebe. I couldn't find a single mention of him.

Will—

I think he's lying.

Well, I don't.

If you were taking up, oh, Buddhism, I wouldn't mind. If you'd decided to collect old coins—

Oh, she said, leaning back. Old coins. Will, if that's what you want, I'll be less of a hobbyist. I have to stop living in sin. No, let me finish. I've waited for God to hand me a revelation, but I don't think that's how He loves us. Hold on. This isn't about you, Will. I've given it a lot of thought. If I did what people here do—if I chased high-paid jobs, and I wrote fifteen-page papers on Milton, I have no idea who that would help. But if I could find out what I am. If I have a soul. I've thought about what St. Augustine said, that we have to beg the Lord to know Him. It wasn't until the 18th century that the church established belief as a precondition of Christian faith—if I act as though I believe, maybe I'll also experience the divine. If I don't, I'll have tried. Isn't that what you did?

She reached across the table, waiting for me to admit that yes, I had. But I was also picturing the two of them in the car's claustral space: a private, long drive, the partial curtain of Phoebe's hair swinging. She laughed, ignoring phone calls. He'd have instructed Phoebe about what to tell me, tonight. It was central to his appeal that he liked giving orders. Is this his idea? I asked.

No.

Did he stay with you last night?

It wasn't, she said. He did, but it's not—

So, let's be honest. This isn't about being a born-again virgin for Christ. It's about you, the wide-eyed acolyte, fucking the guru.

Will, you don't mean this.

Sure, I do. It's what people do in cults like Jejah. You do realize, of course, that it's a cult. That's what's changed, if you're wondering. I wasn't sure, at first, but it's the truth. He's a low-rent Jesus freak with Franciscan affectations. So, how does it work: do you take turns, fucking him, or is it one big orgy, just a giant Christ-loving pile? I wish you'd told me, though. I'd have joined you—

She pushed the cup off the table. A wet stain swelled across the floorboards, broken glass glittering. I'll get it, I said.

Don't, she said, crying. I went to find the broom. When I returned, she was still at the table. I brushed glass into the dust-pan, but the bristles proved too coarse. I wetted paper towels. I daubed up what I could. With each pass, I folded the towels in half until the square was too small to use. A glint caught my eye: a piece had fallen on Phoebe's foot, between the fine-boned toes. I picked it off; she shied.

It was glass, I said.

I don't care.

She went into the bedroom. The slam rattled the toaster oven; its lid fell open. I thought of the short-lived ruckus, years ago, when a Carmenita high-school kid, Jim, had sighted Christ's face in a slice of burned toast. Local papers published photos of the miracle bread, His face almost visible. While, at the time, I credited the apparition, I'd also felt the insult. I believed, of course, that household theophanies took place, visions of the Son of Man spotted in pieces of foil, paint blotches. Spitz dogs' assholes. Crocks of jam. Burned-toast Jesus, though, had shown up less than a mile from where I lived. So, what had moved the Lord to neglect me? Instead, He'd picked this kid, a once-a-month Christian: Jim Struth, who didn't love Him, not as I did. A twinge alerted me to a piece of glass in my thumb. I finished wiping the spill, then I went to the sink to pinch it out.

26.

JOHN LEAL

It wasn't that Christianity fetishized pain, or exalted it. What point could there be in glorifying something so available? It would be like exalting oxygen. But the faith did recognize the potential effect of pain: how it can, with most of us, open what's closed. Like cut flesh, we become available to excluded possibilities. Light enters in the injured place, he said. That the bones which He hath broken might rejoice.

27.

PHOEBE

In the next Jejah confession, Phoebe might have said to them, One night, I walked past a woman talking with a small boy in a white sailing suit. They're waiting, she told him, in Korean. We should rush. The child trotted, obedient, his soles flaring. The woman bent down to kiss the top of his head. I'd stopped in place. I watched them, feral with longing. When a taxi slid past, I wished: Hit them. In pain, I wanted the world to feel as I did. So, Will. Poor Will. Paradise still burns his eyes, but he can't get back in. It would be hard to witness others' faith; he tried so long for his own. Though he's lived in a state of lack, people often take what he's lost to be nothing, a joke. Even his mother still thinks it's a phase. His childish rebellion. He grieves, the absence more vivid to him than what's present, while being forced to pretend he's fine. It's possible that, with time, the mask has sealed itself upon his face.

John Leal says I should stop living with Will. But if I moved, I'd join the list of all those Will loves who failed him. One parent in Florida; the other ill, preoccupied with Christ. The God-shaped hole, Will calls it. He hears the church bells sing, but not to him.

28.

WILL

I exiled myself to the living room. The mattress on the thrift-store futon was so thin that its metal ribs jutted through. I slept on the floor instead, bundled in a plaid blanket. Late the fifth night, finding me like this, Phoebe insisted I come back to bed.

No, I'm all right, I said.

But you're shivering.

She pulled off the blanket; holding it like a cape, she took it to the bedroom. I waited as long as I could before giving in. She'd left my half of the bed unoccupied. Lulled by the shared warmth, I fell asleep. The following night, she started wearing more to bed than her usual cotton panties, adding a shirt, striped pajama pants, the clothed skin radiating heat, but still taboo. I couldn't help imagining Phoebe with him. Paired, they flashed from the ceiling, shining billboard projections of his black-nailed toes fumbling up and down Phoebe's muscled legs. He strained with effort. Thighs lifted to meet him, and he looped my girl-friend's ponytail in his hand. With a hard tug, the way she liked it, he tightened the leash, Phoebe's face shown smooth, fast, as if surging from the pool.

———

One evening, while she was at the Litton Street house, Julian came to the apartment. Will, how do you like Phoebe's new friends? he asked, setting down a cellophane-wrapped ballotin.

I don't, I said. I thought she should see a therapist, but—

It's not something she'd do.

No.

She's being ridiculous. It's not as though she pushed Liesl from that railing. I think it's selfish, all this bogus guilt. It isn't Phoebe's fault that Liesl died. Of course, it's not. She didn't kill Liesl, and her mother died in an L.A. traffic crash. It was an accident. People die. It happens. I blame the sackcloth bigots. Such a bad influence. This isn't an exact parallel, but I'm re-minded of the video artist I used to date, Elvis Floril. No one liked him. Elvis, the moral zero. But he was so talented. Is. I was infatuated. I couldn't listen to what my friends had been telling me, until, like that, I did. The thing is, though, they kept trying.

He was still talking when Phoebe returned home. I hadn't

said much; I didn't tell Julian I had no idea she felt implicated in Liesl's death. I couldn't have admitted that she'd withheld what she'd confided in him, just as she trusted John Leal, taking his side, not mine, all the while picking a fictional God, a parent who died, Liesl—every single person, that is, but me, the Phoebe-loving fool who kept putting her first. But the more I thought about it, well, Julian could be wrong. He'd been Liesl's oldest friend at Edwards. It was possible he ascribed to Phoebe the guilt that he, Julian, felt. If he were right, I'd have noticed.

The next night, I found I'd paused in front of Exhibit, a dive nightclub on Whiting Street that I'd heard Phi Epsilons extol. Like fishing in a kiddie pool, a pledge had said. Inside, spotlit girls pivoted on round tables. I had to push through a pit to get to the bar; when I slipped, the humid bodies, writhing, held me upright. I didn't stay long, but I kept going back until the night I walked a girl, Leigh, from Exhibit to her place. She told me about the spin classes she taught for a living. I was invited in. She pulled off her shirt. Small, tanned packs of abdominal muscle shifted as she fidgeted with a satin bra.

I forgot I—I have to—

I couldn't think of an excuse. The bra, tissue pink, dangled from one strap. I left, apologizing: I went home, where Phoebe slept, sick with the flu. I'd helped her to bed before going out. In the trashcan, I caught sight of the torn plastic of a tampon sheath, and when I crept beneath the blanket, she turned toward me, still unconscious, wrapping me in limbs and warmth, this bleeding, feverish creature I didn't know how to stop wanting.

———

I quit the Exhibit visits. I received an email from Leigh asking if I'd like to get a bite to eat sometime, but I didn't know what to write. One day sped past, then several, until I thought it would be more insulting if I wrote, at this late point, than if I didn't respond at all. The note might have been lost in transit, or she'd written to the wrong Will Kendall.

———

While I still had Phoebe with me, hot in my arms, singing Ella Fitzgerald back to life as I washed the dishes, I knew what I was losing, and it ached as if she'd already gone. The expected rift came in late March. I was home; she planned to have gimlets with Julian at the Colonial. I'd heard his reproaches tolling from Phoebe's earpiece when he called. I miss you, angel, he'd said. *Bix* misses you. He says no one's asked for his house special in ages, and how could you be unkind to Bix?

I was in the kitchen, fixing a salad. I sliced a red onion lengthwise, then into minute squares. I swept the last diced bits off the knife: piled amethysts, I thought, a geode. I had the idea I'd show it to Phoebe. I'd finished most of a bottle of wine. She was in the bedroom, door open, trying to zip up a dress. It was a black shift I liked, and I laughed as I said, I'm coming, I'll help.

She flinched at the sound, but she'd left the door open. It shouldn't have been a surprise that I'd noticed she was changing. She backed up to the wall, bent elbows slanting above her head. No, I can do it, she said. Let me help, I insisted. I'll zip the dress. I spun Phoebe to face the wall, lighthearted, but then I saw that, in the space where the knit dress gaped open, she had a back crisscrossed with welts, bruises. In spots, the skin had broken. Some of the marks had partially healed. Others looked fresh, a dull red. Phoebe, I said. What is this?

She pulled away from me, flushing.

Phoebe, please—

It's nothing.

Who did this to you?

She walked out of the room, and I followed. We sat at the kitchen table. I asked if I should call the police, if she was in pain.

No.

Phoebe, what happened?

She'd tell me, she said. But first, I had to listen. They'd been holding group penances. In turn, they detailed how they'd failed God, then asked the others to help them with physical notes of what they'd resolved. One night, they sang to God while they knelt on uncooked rice grains, hands up until their arms collapsed. They fasted. The flesh is strong; the mind, frail. We believe with our bodies, she said.

She was still in the half-zipped dress, but she'd also thrown a coat on her shoulders, with fawn cashmere so thick and soft that, at parties, I used to be able to reach into a pile of coats and find hers by touch. Its lush cloth wings dangled down. I wish I could explain how helpful he's been, she said. I feel light again. Will, I'm jubilant. I'm glad to be alive. If I could just have you with me, as well—

You haven't enjoyed living, I said.

But you know what I mean. It's the peace that passeth understanding.

Phoebe's smile flared, the old outsize grin. It belonged to someone I'd known. Last fall, caught in a flash storm, we were rushing through Noxhurst when Phoebe's shoe strap broke. I picked her up, but the hold slipped. She laughed, or I did. Legs flailed, fish-bright. The beige raincoat bunched, slid; wet hairs, like blown seaweed, filled my mouth. She writhed, but I held on. I'd carried Phoebe home. She'd left the bedroom door open. It had to be on purpose: she wished me to learn what he'd done.

She joined her hands on the table. I pulled one loose, and I kissed the inside of Phoebe's wrist. The pulse flitted, urgent with life. When I licked the trapped blue of a vein, she shivered. I kissed an eyelid. She lifted open lips, at first, to meet mine. We slid down, the planks cold, but then she stopped responding, mouth rigid. Beneath the kitchen lights, Phoebe's face was a mask of gold. It hid the living girl. If I could crack it apart—she pushed herself up, sitting cross-legged, and I saw the logical solution, so simple I wanted to laugh. I told Phoebe we should get married.

You're joking, she said.

No.

I watched as she realized I was serious. I think, she said, Will, I—

Phoebe—

I'm late for Julian, and you've had a few drinks—we'll talk about this in the morning, when you'll—

Since I didn't want to let Phoebe refuse, I pushed my mouth on hers again. The shift dress had come loose. Bra-strap nicks, like the lines dividing a doll's joints, indented Phoebe's skin. It's possible she struggled awhile before I noticed she wasn't, as I thought, excited, but I'd waited a long time. If I pretended I didn't understand, I could postpone letting go. The fitted bottom half of Phoebe's dress had twisted at waist-level. With my body pressing hers down, I could easily move the panties aside, unzip my jeans. Stop, she said; I slipped inside. She went still. I finished, then I went to the bathroom. I locked myself in.

I woke the next morning on the bathroom mat. She'd left the apartment. I went outside, too. I walked until it was night; I called her, leaving messages, apologies I couldn't finish. What you crying about, pal, a man said, panhandling. Take this soda bottle, drink it all up like Lou Reed, baby. He rattled his plastic cup, and laughed. I knew where she'd be. In three nights, she called back to tell me she'd return home Sunday, at noon, but just to finish moving out. Jejah had a room available.

It shouldn't take long, she said. I'm asking you to stay out of the apartment until I'm done. I don't want to see you.

She hung up. I went out for a walk again. Rain fell, melting winter's ice. Sidewalks broke, heaved, oozing months-old grit. In this newly liquid world, other natural laws might also prove flexible. Time, I'd learned, was believed to be less sequential than it felt. It could spiral; it frilled. It might well halt. Then, it was the next morning. Night followed, but I still had time. Rivulets sluiced into the gutters, sailing trash, and then it was the Sabbath, almost noon. I waited until past midnight, sitting at the bar at Exhibit, before I returned to the apartment. When I stepped inside, I could tell she'd gone. She'd left the furniture, but book-shelf spaces gaped open. In the closet, stripped hangers clattered. She hadn't taken the peacock silk wrap I liked, a gift from Julian. It could be a sign: a daedal thread, the implied promise of return. I'd had too much to drink. Stumbling, I went to bed.

I opened my eyes, and I'd sprawled in a jut of sunlight, floating in the usual daze of a headache. Not quite conscious, I reached toward Phoebe, and I felt the cold of taut cotton. It was the white sheet, its lip folded on top of the blanket, Phoebe's side of the bed pulled flat.

29.

JOHN LEAL

He often prayed, he said, about the old man who leaned on his cane at the clinic exit, eyes lifted. When asked what he was doing, he explained he was counting the souls of slaughtered babies. Rising to the Lord, the old man said. The angel babies rise on high. He was right, John Leal said. I looked up until I saw them, too. Spirits, a long line floating toward the Lord. In each child's name, praise Him. We'll devote the revolution to these short lives, and He will, in turn, lift His face upon us.

30.

PHOEBE

I've lied about the crash, Phoebe then told them. That night, in L.A., we did watch a cellist. I'd been crying, and I insisted on driving us home from the concert hall. Blinded, I lost control of the sedan: all this, I've admitted. I also said, though, that she died at once. She didn't. I hit the truck, then the sedan slid along a railing. It flipped on its side. The next time I opened my eyes, she'd fallen on top of me. I asked if she was hurt. She didn't respond, but she was still breathing. People outside kept shouting that the metal had twisted. They'd have to slice it open. But I had both hands free. I'd heard the stories about people finding inborn superhuman abilities, lifting cars to save trapped babies. I tried to push. It had no effect. She'd moved fast to put herself between me and the truck. In that split of time, she'd unbuckled the seat belt. She'd hurled in front of me. If she could do all that, I should at least be able to help pull us out. Instead, I sat in place. I waited while she bled to death.

John's said that Christ is with us, not beyond, in pain. To recall those I've hurt, to catalog the times I've failed, is also to learn how to forgive. Christ's purifying crucible isn't pain, but sin. Each loss includes its redress; each evil, its pardon. The truth is, I did crash. People lift cars. I claim this guilt. If all is possible for those who believe, if I, if you, can be so much at fault, think how powerful you and I will be.

31.

WILL

With April rolling into spring, I tried one more time. I read all the advice I could find for people hoping to pull those they loved from cults. I emailed Tess, the girl who'd quit the group just before I joined, but the note couldn't be delivered: she'd left school, I gathered. I attempted to enlist Julian, as well. He didn't return my calls, so I borrowed a Phi Epsilon's jeep. I drove to Litton Street, to the Jejah house.

I intended to apologize, in person; as the literature advised, I wanted to let Phoebe know I could be depended upon. Full, positive support, but once I parked, I didn't get out. The windshield sprouted buds of light rain. In a little while, I thought, but still the minutes ticked past. When I looked at my watch again, it was almost midnight, too late to ring the bell. I kept seeing the point in time, and choice, when I pressed Phoebe down against the floorboards. She'd flinched with pain, then surprise. I'd found it satisfying: I enjoyed frightening the girl I loved. I had hurt Phoebe more than they could. I wasn't to be trusted. If I loved Phoebe, I'd leave the girl alone. Useless tears burned my eyes. I left when I could.

———

I sent Julian a note with what I'd learned about cults, after which, knowing Phoebe's schedule, I did as she asked, staying away. With no sign of Phoebe, I kept finding I'd paused to gaze, instead, at a beige raincoat thrown across a bench; a girl in a striped dress. The dining-hall grand piano, its glossed lid hinged open. Piped-in Ella, scatting, had me at a standstill in the deli aisle. The bathtub drain clogged. I pulled out a black plug, the tangled hairs iridescent with soap-froth. She'd left lip balm in a pile of toiletries. I twisted open the black cap: the gel surface was still indented, rough with use. I inhaled the faint salt scent of Phoebe's mouth, then sealed the balm. I put it beneath the sink, where I could find it.

By chance, in late April, I saw Phoebe again. I was exiting the dining hall. In the rotunda, I saw my old girlfriend walking in. It was too late to pretend otherwise. Once we'd said hello, she fell silent. Others hurried past. She stood in place, face averted, until, at a loss, I asked about Julian.

Julian, she said.

Your friend, I said. Julian Noh. Tall. Korean.

I haven't talked to him in a while.

I looked up, startled. I'd gotten used to the sound of Phoebe on the phone with him, the Julian who also stopped by without notice, pint of kimchi in hand, illegal Czech absinthe. He'd leave the gift in the kitchen before he hightailed it into the bedroom, taking hours of Phoebe's time. But you love Julian, I said.

She shifted an arm, a one-sided shrug. The rotunda light whitened Phoebe's features as in an overexposed photo, already turning this, us, into the past. I apologized; she interrupted, head shaking. I should go, she said. Will, I don't think you've even tried to understand—

I caught sight of Phoebe one more time, that spring. She was crossing the quadrangle with John Leal, lit up then extinguished in pools of light. I watched Phoebe laugh. She had on a jacket I didn't recognize: his, perhaps. It hid her small frame. I turned left; I let them be.

————

In June, I moved south, to Manhattan, for a hedge-fund internship. I worked long hours, more than I had in Beijing, but I didn't mind. In fact, I solicited extra projects. I couldn't fill what little time alone I had. I required pills, or alcohol, often both, to fall asleep. Nights, I was in the habit of spilling the bottle of prescribed sedatives onto the bedside table to look at the pills scattered white, like dice. I'd made the novice mistake of living downtown, next to the fund. The Financial District emptied along with its office buildings. I drifted the streets in the milk heat of late mornings. Taxis blurred past, roof lights signaling isolation.

One evening, as I walked home from the office, I saw a girl stumble, then fall. Leaning toward the curb, she threw up. I'd have kept walking, but she'd drawn people's attention. Someone whistled, laughing. A group of loud men stopped to watch, swaying in place like a barbershop quartet. I bent down, telling the girl my name. I asked if she knew where she was going.

I'm in a hotel, she said. It has a café called the Black Spotted Dog. The White Dog. I don't know. It has no dogs. My girlfriends—

She threw up again, gasping. Unsure what else to do, I held back the girl's bob, thin curls clinging with sweat. She asked for water, her voice small. The tinted glass of a deli reflected our images. I went in. I bought a bottle of Evian. I handed it to the girl, and, still sitting, she tried a sip, spat it out, then poured the rest of the bottle on her head. Liquid gushed down the girl's dress, splashed the tan slopes of slim legs. Holding the upended bottle, she wept.

Exhausted, I helped the girl up. Lukewarm Evian rilled through my hands as in the baptismal rites I'd loved, and I recalled my mother's smile rising from the lake, light striating the muddied blue. Phoebe pushing herself out of the pool, the wet flashing down in sheets. Medieval penitents so avid for holiness they'd swilled saints' baths, a long tradition of lustral mania that led straight to the penitential cuts striping Phoebe's back. Was this also faith's aftereffect, the lingering taste for others' histrionics? If so, I'd had enough.

Where's your hotel? I asked, about to hail a taxi.

She named an intersection close to the seaport, a couple of blocks north. I could walk you there, I offered.

She stopped crying, and stared. I don't think so, she said.

But I, those drunks are watching you, and—

Who the hell are you?

I provided my name again, but she recoiled, flinging off the arm with which I held her up. She thrust both palms out, a warning, as she backed down the street, toward the hotel. I stayed where I was. In the days to come, I couldn't forget that storefront glass, the mirrored girl. This girl wasn't Phoebe, I realized that, but I kept seeing a procession of girls falling down, long hair radiating into black haloes. In half-zipped shift dresses, they hold out a hand. I lift the girls up, unhurt: I watch them go.

———

In the fall, back at Edwards, I was at a Phi Epsilon social when I heard from a friend of Julian's that Phoebe was home, in Los Angeles. She'd taken the term off from school. Unspecified personal reasons, the friend said. I excused myself, and I went to the bathroom. I sat on a tub, breathing. I hadn't realized I was waiting to be given news. It sounded as though she'd quit Jejah. Maybe Phoebe's father had learned the truth about his gulag charlatan. He'd swept in to help. I left the social without talking to anyone else; I didn't want to dilute the joy I felt.

Then, in October, I was invited by Nikhil Mehta, a Phi Epsilon, to watch the airball game from his suite. I'd been secluded in a library carrel, finishing midterm papers; but the sun, like mild alcohol, had me longing to be with people, life. Blue flags flicked, the wind thin, rustling. In minutes, students would fill the lawn, fighting to help hit an inflated, six-foot ball toward the goal. I imagined the Edwards ghosts drawn to this sport, an old college tradition; they'd have sniffed the blood. I walked to Nikhil's place while they pushed close, thirsting to live again. Wraiths plucked my sleeve. It couldn't be helped. But is all this just in hindsight, or did burned slips of carbon drift past at the time, ash singeing my nostrils? I can't stop thinking about what, if anything, I suspected. If there are parts I could have forestalled. I climbed five flights up Wyeth Hall. Soon, I was sitting in a windowsill, drink in hand. Nikhil sat next to me.

—in disguises? a girl asked him. She straddled the sill to his left, swinging a leg: she'd leaned toward him to be heard across the party's noise.

We're still talking about this? he said.

It's all I can think about.

But that's the problem.

They said more. I'd stopped listening. Behind us, I heard the light pop of a wine bottle opening. I thought I should get up to refill my glass, but I was unwilling to lose the sill. The airball inflated. Students crowded the lawn. They reached up, hundreds of open hands trying to swat the globe. Shouts swelled with each change in direction. The ball bounced, and rose: the beige sphere gleaming, a downed sun. It fell, then rolled. It soared again.

—in thinking they're doing good, Nikhil said. Still, those girls' deaths had to be an accident. It has to be the reason no one's taking credit for the clinics. The bombers must have been pro-life, though I don't like using that term—

I broke in. What clinics, I said. They both turned to me, astonished. I think I'd guessed while I asked. But as though I hadn't, or as if, by pretending, I'd change a truth I didn't want, I repeated the question.

———

I stayed long enough to establish that the girls who died had been identified as five local high-school students, and then I left Nikhil's suite. Pausing at a newsstand, I bought papers. I scanned headlines while I walked. On Mitchell Street, a block from home, a van almost hit me. It swerved right, honking.

In the apartment, I opened my laptop. Hands shaking, I had

to keep retyping search terms, but then I pulled up the news. Friday night, at 8:00, explosions had leveled five women's health clinics in New York State, including in Noxhurst. The clinics had all provided abortions. Each clinic was the sole occupant of a building with an open parking lot. Initial reports indicated that truck bombs had been left next to load-bearing walls. The five girls belonged to a cheerleading squad. They'd been in the wide Noxhurst lot, practicing a routine, when the bomb exploded. Bodies had been retrieved, the girls' involvement ruled out. With the repeated fives, it sounded fictitious, like the lead-in to a bad joke. I'd been alone in the carrel, studying. How hadn't I heard about this, Nikhil had said. Didn't I read the news, what had I been doing—

My phone had died, so I called Phoebe from the landline, a candy-red vintage rotary phone she'd found years ago in a Paris street market. I picked it up. It felt solid, reliable. Even the handset had weight. We'd installed the line in case I was needed at home while I had the cell phone on silent, since I was always afraid I'd miss a late-night call. Phoebe had objected, at first, but then she produced this shining relic.

You should have seen it when I bought it, she'd said, with pride, showing me the scratches she'd filled in, the extra polish. It had taken a long time to find a glaze that matched. She loved this phone. I was surprised she'd left it behind. Now, I noticed I'd let dust muddle its high gloss. I rubbed it with my shirt. But she was in Los Angeles. No one could fix a phone like this, then blow up five clinics.

The call didn't go through, and it occurred to me the landline couldn't dial long-distance numbers. I plugged in the cell phone. When it blinked on, I called Phoebe. I left a message. Talk to me, I said. Please. I waited, then I tried again.

32.

JOHN LEAL

If he could, he'd admit that, at times, it wasn't simple. They'd pledged to fight in the service of the living God, and he'd learned to accept that faith is not a gift. It is not the object you receive intact, at once, by putting out a hand. Though long streamers of sunlight might fawn at his feet, faith came as the hard-won reward, battle spoils he wrested from the heaped debris. The wars to come would be a divine healing, in which the pure would not be killed.

33.

PHOEBE

The first time I played music for anyone else, Phoebe said, it was to audition with a well-known soloist. He didn't think he wanted a child student, but one of my mother's friends had urged him to give me a trial. Until then, I'd had no lessons: I sat at the piano because I loved what I could do. He stacked books on his bench. I climbed up, then I played as I always had. I stopped when the soloist pressed his hands into his eyes. I thought that, disliking what I'd done, he hoped to avoid looking at me. I didn't care. I wasn't sure I wanted the instruction; it felt artificial, like being taught to breathe. But then, he put his hands down, and I saw he was crying. He asked what I thought while I hit the keys. I told him that sound was trapped in the piano. I had to let it out.

So, you've heard the piano's soul shining through, he said.

I couldn't tell, at the time, what he meant. Now, though, I think he was right. It's taken me a long while to recall what I was born knowing. I've visited the old Hilcox Street graves. People in those days died more often as infants, often within the first month of life. I've written down the inscriptions of children who barely lived. I'll recite the names. What I've learned from grief is how superficial it is. I'm tired of being selfish. I had the single plea: Lord, I'm in pain. But I want to be useful. I'll delight in God's will, which is His grace toward me. If I act with faith, I don't have to be afraid.

DAVID FITCH	ELIJAH GIRD	NATHANIEL HOLLIN
SYBIL DAVIS	DANIEL HALL	JOEL BARTGIS
EZRA CATLIN	J. T. BRINTNAL	FIELDING BLAUVELT
JOHN GIBB	ELIPHELET LADD	GAIL LUNT
LOUIS WHITING	JULIET FALTIX	JABEZ BOYD GILBERT
MERIT WYETH	RUTH YUNDT	ETHEL KIRK
GILBERT MERRILL	HEZEKIAH DAVIS	TITUS MARTIN
SARAH ELLIS	LEVI TALBOT	MILES KEITH
CHRISTOPH POULSON	MERIT LAHN	OBADIAH PECHIN
MATTHIAS HILCOX	JOHAN PURNELL	FAITH HOYT PRATT
PHILIP STILSON	ITHIEL TODD	RICHARD WELLS
MARION COIT	HAVILA FAUST	PHILIP NEWHALL
JULES DUCLOT	T. I. HOYT FEIT	ETTA MYGATT
ISAIAH PIERSON	NEWTON LANG	LUCIUS ALBIG
PHINEAS ALBIG	HORATIO COTTELL	PHILA HOYT
ELIPHELET BALL	DANIEL PLATT	JOHN LYALL
MABEL LANG	FRANCIS JOSEPH COIT	MILES EVANS

NAOMI HOYLAND	BAVIL KING	ELIHU GILL
JOSIAH MEIGS	MARIAH HALL	SYBIL BUEL
IRVING PLATT	ITHIEL BUEL	J. D. STILES
ELIHU RINEHART	ISAAC ALBURTIS	FRANTZ BOYD
BENJAMIN CHILTON	JOEL BOYD	LORING ALLEN
EZRA LEVITT	LYDIA GIBB	GAIL FAUST
FRANCIS STILES	MERIT TODD	PHILA FALTIX
WILLIAM INGERSOLL	EDWARD HOPKINS	JULIET LUNT

34.

WILL

I stayed up through much of the night, not getting in bed until the curtain edges had lightened with morning. By noon, she still hadn't called. The extended silence, though, left me less anxious than I'd felt, not more. Much as I might want to talk, I'd lost that right months ago. She'd been home all along, in L.A. I could imagine Phoebe lazing poolside, beneath a hat brim's flopping petal. If her phone rattled, she ignored it. Ripe oranges plopped. I'd have a birthday soon, I realized. It was in less than a week. The last time, I'd had trouble convincing Phoebe I didn't want a celebration: no big gathering, I said. No barhopping expedition. She thought awhile, then proposed I at least take a short trip. I asked what she had in mind.

Rolling to face me, she said, What about Coney Island?

Oh, so you want to go to Coney Island.

You'll love it.

I drove us down to the lowest tip of Brooklyn. I was put off, at first: its kitsch, the noise. Then, I had a couple of beers. She led me to pinball and tilt-a-whirls, to a sideshow stall. We spun in teacups. Toddlers squalled; clowns tottered past on painted, salt-glazed stilts. Street acrobats flung up agile legs. Ignoring the fall chill, girls on the beach lolled in bikinis, flat bared stomachs shining like mirrors to the sun. Night fell, and Phoebe and I split blini and horseradish-infused vodka. The plucked flesh of rose petals strewed the tablecloth. She tapped out the birthday song on the inside of my thigh. In the past, I hadn't understood what made people flag birthdays, let alone with parties—celebrating death's advent, I thought. Meanwhile, glittering Coney Island was what I'd wanted. I hadn't known, but she had. This time, I waited. The phone didn't ring until late in the morning with my mother's hello, barely audible.

Is this a good time for you, Will?

It is.

We talked, and she told me she'd started a new job. It was one, then two, three, four; then five; then six o'clock. The doorbell rang. In a rush, I dropped my glass, but it was Leigh, looking uncertain. You don't like birthdays, fine, she said. She held out a round tin, fingernails polished red. But even you have to like a fresh rhubarb tart.

It isn't a good time, I should have explained, but I asked if she wanted to come in. When Phoebe moved out last spring, I'd run into Leigh again, at Exhibit; since then, we'd shared a bed often enough that she might have expected to see me once I'd returned to Noxhurst. It's been hectic, with school, I said, pouring the cask-strength bourbon I knew she liked. Ice slid in the glass. I meant to call, but I've had a lot going on.

No, I figured. I just thought you could use a treat.

I crouched to clean the gin I'd spilled. The glass had broken into several clean shards. Still, I wiped around the spot in case I missed a piece, and I thought of Phoebe, yes, but I was also recalling an earthquake I'd lived through when I was five, six. I'd squatted beneath the dining-room table while plates leaped from the shelves, white fragments like giant teeth gnashing toward us. With my mother's arms around me, I felt how frightened she was, her breaths fast, but she'd sung to me, an upbeat Bizet tune with improvised English lyrics. She kept singing, heroic, to help me be less fearful, until the convulsions stopped. If I'd truly believed life began at minute zero—

What is it? Leigh said.

It's nothing.

I waited until she left, then I tried one last call. Phoebe's father's house was listed; he, too, had a landline. He picked up, to my surprise. I'd all but forgotten that dialing a phone could result in a live conversation. I asked for Phoebe. She's at Edwards, he said.

No, she isn't, I almost said. Instead, I ended the call. I had no reason to trust him. He'd introduced them in the first place.

When his office opened in the morning, I went to see Dean Pasch, the head of my hall. I waited; I looked out the window at a girl sporting a cowboy hat. She sat on the courtyard's split-rail fence, talking with someone who, as I watched, pushed his hand beneath the back of her shirt. He moved up in slow circles. His forearm bulged from the girl's spine, distending ribbed cloth until he exposed a tall swath of freckled skin. She should have stopped him. If I could forget about Phoebe, I'd spirit the girl away from here. To a ranch, I thought, out West, with no neighbors for miles. We'd raise a passel of freckled children, bringing them up on Plato, sunlight, and backyard peaches. I was called into Pasch's office. I hadn't seen him since the previous fall, when he'd helped with a hitch in my scholarship funding, but he saluted me by name. He asked what he might do for me.

The doorbell chimed the next morning. It's Phoebe, I thought, pulling on clothes, but this time I opened the door to four people. The president of Edwards, Pasch, and two people I didn't recognize. Federal agents, they said. Fitz and Hugh. They swept past me, into the hall. It sounded like a carnival act, topping the playbill: the famed traveling duo. With such names, they couldn't be serious. The woman agent, Fitz or Hugh, said I should take a seat. If I kept standing, I'd obstruct the investigation. I hesitated.

Sit down, she said.

I let Pasch lead me to the futon. President Wright joined us. More strangers piled in, filling the small apartment. With Pasch, in his office, I'd explained that Phoebe couldn't have bombed the clinics. In fact, I'd heard she was home, in California. But it didn't seem to be the case. Well, she could be anywhere. I didn't want to make wild claims. She wasn't here, though, at school. If she was with Jejah, she might be in trouble. I had no specifics. This will sound trivial, I said, but Phoebe wouldn't let a birthday pass without getting in touch. She'd at least have sent a note.

It doesn't sound trivial, Pasch had said.

The strangers packed books into bins. Photos, too. The laptop. Puerh tea, then a half-eaten gochujang tin. I'd tried advertising the living-room space, but I hadn't found an applicant I liked. I should have moved, but she loved this place. She'd picked it out while I was in Beijing. I couldn't have left, not if she might return. Instead, I continued paying the doubled rent. Now, I watched people upend the place, a life I'd kept intact.

In the bathroom, an agent opened the cabinet. I saw him shift toiletries into a bin, and then I was at the sink, as well. He'd taken Phoebe's lip balm, the black plastic lid like a button. I fished it from the box. I heard the agent tell me to put it down. But there had to be a limit. While I recognized the lip balm wasn't mine, it also wasn't his. When he tried to grab it, I dodged past him. I began to run, though I wasn't sure where I'd go. I was flat-footed; I had no shoes on. Phoebe had prohibited shoes inside the apartment: think of where those soles have been, she'd said, citing bacilli, dog shit, public-bathroom tiles, until I shared the bias, but now I couldn't run.

I hadn't crossed the living room before I was jerked back, a hand seizing my wrist. It tried to prize out the balm. I flailed; my heel hit something soft, and then I fell.

35.

JOHN LEAL

He'd lain down with his followers in the clearing. Birds darted left, then right, stitching a hole. The blue expanse might have been a colossal rip in the partition between the group and His plan. If only, he thought. If God had been that visible, His objectives so plain. Instead, even with him, God fell silent until John Leal had to fill in the absence: to speak, like this, in His place.

I know, he said, that you want me to tell you what comes next. That you might feel confused, even frightened. The truth is—but he paused. He sat up, looking into the open, perturbed faces. The truth. They'd each come to him broken, desperate for healing. Since pain takes changing forms, he tried to be what his people needed. In short, he'd reshaped himself in his disciples' image. He picked up a handful of dirt. The soft, fine soil, silted from Christ's blood. He glanced at the sky, now emptied. With a sigh, he upended his hand. The hole was left unsewn. The truth is—

36.

PHOEBE

While I look for the Lord, I've found Him. If I lift a stone, I'll
see Him beneath it. Cut a tree open, and I'll have Him again.
I've thought so often, Phoebe said, of the idea that longing
should be allowed the chance to find its object. Since desire
pleads to have more, I'll inhabit that space. It's a privilege to
have loved: with each loss, I've gained practice in the divine. I
haven't given up loving my mother just because she died. If she'd
taken a trip, the love wouldn't end. It's not so different, except
that I haven't known when, and if, she'll return. But the Lord
moves in the rifts. He fills the void. To the extent that I can be
present with a want of the Lord, I'll be with Him, too.

37.

WILL

Growing up, I watched people try to ruin their own lives. In Carmenita, kids melted skin with polluted tattoos. They'd drive while high, headlamps unlit, in pursuit of invisibility. Haile Nichol, a friend's cousin, had been dancing with lit sparklers in her mouth when she tripped. One slid down her throat. She died spitting light. Shooting potato guns, vandalizing police cars, they drag-raced in gullies and picked fights with giants—they, I'd have said, but here I was, in jail, sitting chained to a metal table: a child of Carmenita, bona fide. My head throbbed. I'd hit it, falling, when I ran. I still hadn't been allowed a phone call. The door opened with a click, then Fitz and Hugh walked in.

It turned out the man was Hugh; the woman, Fitz. Sitting first, eyes bright, Fitz leaned forward. I shouldn't ask how you're feeling, she said. Because, well, you did kick Agent Hugh in the stomach while tainting federal evidence, and that's just in the past six hours. You're in trouble, Will, but even so, I don't want you in pain. Would you like medical attention?

I didn't respond. I was afraid to ask if I could have the phone call I should have been allowed. If I wasn't getting that call, I didn't know what else I'd be denied, which basic rights I'd find withdrawn. Fitz said that she'd also studied at Edwards. Ten years before I had. Was that surprising? It was how she'd met President Wright. They'd stayed in touch. She talked about life as a scholarship student, how long it had taken to adjust from Biloxi to Noxhurst. It was a fishing town, Biloxi. Down South. Tourists loved it. I couldn't listen; I had blood singing in my ears, but then she used Phoebe's name.

—Phoebe, the religious fanatics who might be behind the biggest attack on U.S. soil since 9/11, an act, to use plain English, of terrorism. Still, we appreciate what you did, telling Pasch what you suspected. That's good, Will. If Phoebe belongs to a group of terrorists—

But she's not a terrorist, I said.

Go on.

Though I'd intended to stay quiet, this was too big a mistake, one I could fix. She wouldn't risk hurting people, I said. He might have kept Phoebe with him; she could be captive, even, but if I thought she was involved—

I stopped, but she nodded, calm. If you thought she helped

with the clinic bombings, you wouldn't have said a thing, she said. I get it. I have people I love, too, but what's worrying me is the prospect of additional bombs. Will, I don't believe they'd plan to stop at five. If I thought like them, I'd keep going. I'd aim at glory. I bet you would, too. More lives might well be at risk. You could save them.

I kept silent. The room then slowed, pitching. Lights brightened, and a hand lifted my head, slanting it until Hugh's broad face sprang into sight. He looked mild, almost solicitous, even as his hand crashed down again. Panic flared; my head swung left. Dazed, blind, I heard Fitz's voice whistling through.

Will, here's a secret I shouldn't tell you. We've received hundreds of tips, paranoid citizens pointing fingers in every direction. I've heard earfuls about hijab-clothed Muslim neighbors. Sufis. Jehovah's Witnesses. The town socialist. It's a problem, to be honest. Do you think we're all here because you had a hunch about an old girlfriend who's gone missing? No. We'd want physical evidence. Film, for instance. Security-camera stills from the clinic showing each Jejah person's face. Each, perhaps, but Phoebe's. I've learned a lot about this cult, but not like you did. Will, if you think Phoebe's not involved in the attacks, I'm inclined to think you're right. But if you believe what you're telling us, don't you want to help find them?

The side of my face tickled. I touched it: I was bleeding. Once, in a Noxhurst club, Phoebe had straddled a mechanical bull, violating the posted rules by having it dialed to the highest setting. Torso flinging back and forth, she'd swung a hand high. When thrown, she yelled, as though in pain, and I pushed through the crowd to find Phoebe sitting up, a jean-leg rolled. Blood curled down the injured limb, like a prize ribbon. Let's do it again, she said.

I told Fitz I wanted to help. I was allowed a phone at last, so I dialed Paul. He sent a friend, Piero Neri, as counsel, but that wasn't why I gave in. Not to placate Hugh, nor to avoid jail, prosecution. I wanted to be right about Phoebe; Fitz made it possible. If you believe what you're telling us, she'd said.

Fitz requested every detail I had. Begin with how you met, she said. I'll figure out what's relevant. I was hoarse, throat stinging, by the time she said I could go home. She'd be in touch. Until then, she said, you'll have to stop trying to contact Phoebe. It's important. Will, I'm being a friend to you. I'm asking you to promise.

During the following week, while I attended classes and counted baccalà fillets, I was always waiting until I could resume the real life I had online, staring into the laptop I'd borrowed, a glass ball of potential news. I held gin in my left hand; with the right, I kept clicking. One evening, I read about a Noxhurst mosque that had just been vandalized, a U.S. flag painted on the lawn, pipe bombs lobbed through its windows. Most of the ill-assembled pipes had fizzled without exploding, but a single bomb had erupted in the mosque's front hall. Some local bigot, people assumed. Since no one plausible had claimed responsibility for the clinic bombings, anti-Muslim sentiment was running high.

I showed up ahead of time to my next shift at Michelangelo's. Finding Paul, I asked if he had questions about how I'd ended up in jail. He was inspecting shellfish deliveries. Without looking up, he said, So, the kid thinks I want to quiz him. Couple hours in jail, ta-da, you think it makes you fascinating. What am I, the fucking paparazzi?

He slit open a box of live crayfish, and I said I thought he should be kept apprised of what I'd done. Since I work here, I said.

I've told you bozos, he said, I'm up to date with all that needs knowing about you. You've got a secret that affects this place, if it's my business, then I'll be up to date. But this, first off, it's no secret, and also I don't give a shit.

Hand-sized, a spot of red throbbed past, the new hostess's zodiac tattoo. It veiled the side of her neck. The last girl had quit in less than a month. I pushed ahead, telling Paul that maybe he should give a shit, since it was possible I'd dated a girl who, well, if any of this became public knowledge, guests might—but before I could finish, he slapped the bar top, his rings clinking zinc. The crayfish he'd pulled out lifted its petaled tail; he took it up by its midsection, dropped it in the box.

Kendall, I tell you I've got no questions, it means I've got no questions, he said. You think you know a thing I don't? Let me tell you what happened the month those towers fell, when a pack of drunk kids chased the wife with a pistol, yelling, Muslim, go home. The wife's from fucking Sevilla, she's no Muslim, just because she likes to tan in the salons these kids think they'll decide who belongs. I don't give a fuck what you do outside this place. Got it? But what I do care about, what makes this laissez-faire ass of mine pinch tight, I care so much, is that I've worked in this business since I was knee-high to a shitball, but you think I'd set you up with Piero with no clue what I'm doing. You think I'm stupid?

No, I said.

Is that right?

I don't think you're stupid.

Bravo, kid, he said. He patted my face, his palm brine-scented. Go be useful. Tell Joel I'll come in to talk in five.

When I returned to the dining room, Paul was in high spirits, gossiping about the new hire, who, he professed, had worked in fetish porn films. I'm almost certain, he said. It's possible it makes this girl a more skillful hostess, but then again it's possible it doesn't, so you'll have to watch the girl extra close, Kendall. He was riffing about challenging sexual positions when I interrupted him.

Paul, you don't mean this, I said.

He chuckled, glancing at his phone. What's that? he asked.

I appreciate what you said about, I'm grateful—Piero helped,

Paul, but the way everyone here talks about women, I don't think it's respectful. They keep quitting.

Tilting back on his heels, Paul smiled. I thought I was about to lose the job; instead, he said, It's cute. The child's speaking up. I'll give you a tip, though. If you're hoping to wipe down that soul of yours, do it on your own time. Don't fucking waste mine.

———

One night, months ago, I'd called Phoebe, and she kept answering, but without saying a word. I heard what sounded like static; I strained to recognize faint, mingled voices. I thought I could make out Phoebe's, and I was frantic to think she might be injured, trying to respond but unable to talk. I hollered, asking anyone to tell me what was going on. But it was just Phoebe's hip, picking up. I had the idea, at last, of calling others: Julian, Liesl, until I had Phoebe on the line again. What were you so worried about? she asked, laughing. Oh, *Will*. You're a lunatic. I'm fine, you poor thing. I'll be home in a little while.

———

The following evening, unable to face the long hours of searching online, I invited Leigh to the apartment. We sat down to stir-fried bigoli, I burned my mouth with a pull of gin, and I talked. Leigh listened, eyes filling. She stayed the night, but then, in two days, when she turned up on the doorstep without notice, I thought I'd made a mistake: I'd led the girl to expect more than I could give. The bell pealed, and I threw on a shirt, but it was Leigh. She surged up in front of me, papers in hand.

I ran straight here, she panted. Flapping newsprint at me like a broken wing, she told me that, as she passed the Ledig Street kiosk, she'd noticed Phoebe's name in bold print on the front pages.

I took the papers, which showed a blurred photo of a girl who looked like Phoebe, in a baseball cap, the thin face angling up. Puzzled, I examined the picture. In it, a black-haired pony-tail curled through the adjustable slot, but Phoebe disliked how she looked in hats. Unless it was so cold that she had no choice, she didn't use hats, let alone baseball caps.

What's this? I said.

It's a picture from the Noxhurst clinic. The parking-lot camera. Will, they're saying she planted the explosives. The ones at Phipps clinic.

Well, that's not right.

You should look at this.

I read the article. It didn't mention John Leal, let alone his cult. It said that, in the video, the girl in the baseball cap walked up to the clinic, then glanced at the camera. She'd been identified as Phoebe Haejin Lin, an Edwards student. The next morning, five additional Jejah cultists were named, including a new person I didn't recognize: all suspects, but Phoebe was still the principal culprit implicated in the Noxhurst clinic explosions, and so in the five girls' deaths.

The following manhunt elicited false leads in Philadelphia, then Lihue. In Detroit. Slidell. La Paz. The abandoned house where they'd stayed was discovered sixty miles north of Noxhurst, a shingled rental cabin in a birch clearing. News stations looped its photo. The cabin was still front-page news by the time I received a three-line note from Phoebe. From Fitz, that is, since federal agents had intercepted the mail, opening it. Not long afterward, Reverend Lin, Phoebe's father, issued his public statement. He explained he'd donated to the extremist cult that called itself Jejah. He'd given his personal savings, as well as, with his board's approval, church funds.

I believed it to be an organization with peaceful aims, he said, reading. To all those who have been hurt, I beg pardon.

He gripped a white page, his hands fists. His chin, like Phoebe's, ended in a point. Tight-jawed, he jutted it out. It was my first time seeing the man. Phoebe hadn't displayed photos of him. I blamed him; of course, I did. I'd heard the stories. If he'd been less brutish to his then-wife, wouldn't Phoebe have felt less alone? But also, I thought, if I'd failed less. If and if again. He said nothing in his speech about having received a message from his child. He didn't want to mention it, perhaps. It was possible, too, that he wasn't allowed. The police, maybe Fitz, had told him not to. If Phoebe had written to me, she'd have sent him a note, as well. In spite of his faults, she had old-fashioned notions about filial duties, his parental rights. That said, if she hadn't written to him, it could also be a sign. I called his house. He didn't pick up, but I was relieved. It had been a mistake, calling. I'd talk to him in person, I decided. I bought a flight to Los Angeles.

38.

JOHN LEAL

—the truth is, he told them, they were just getting started.

39.

PHOEBE

One of the earliest memories I have takes place in L.A. While I slept, she noticed we had no milk. It was still the two of us. She'd run out to buy it, she decided. The store was down the block. It shouldn't take long. I woke up when she'd gone. I called out, expecting the usual hello; instead, for the first time, I heard solitude. I rushed around the house, but she wasn't to be found. I tiptoed, and I realized I could reach the front doorknob. I'm not sure, though, if this isn't just a tale I've been told: at this point, I slide inside my mother's head, then I watch as she did. Milk jug in hand, I listen to a high, distant wail—a child's, I think, but it isn't until I've left the store that I start to laugh, astonished. I forget the milk. I let it fall. I throw both arms open to this wild child, flying toward me.

40.

WILL

I rented a station wagon at the airport, then I drove to Phoebe's father's church. It was a fifteen-mile drive, with the traffic as hectic as I'd always, in the L.A. I invented, believed it would be. I found the church doors locked, its parking lot vacant. I punched the back wall, several times, until I opened skin. Knuckles burning, I got in the station wagon; I drove toward Reverend Lin's house. It wasn't the Sabbath, but still, with his sizable parish, the church should have been open—

I parked several houses down from his. The street was quiet, lined with palm trees and tidied hedges. In the pale light, the lawns floated wide, like magic carpets, and I thought of Phoebe living here in the months before Edwards, grieving. She'd longed to escape; as had I, but here I was, still so God-haunted.

I walked on blackened palm fronds, a tangled pile: I imagined lifting up the lush jumble of leaves and finding it was Phoebe's hair, disheveled with morning. The stem of a frond shone as white as the part of her head. She'd raise a hand, then drop it, unwilling. I'd tease her out of bed since, having had the night apart, I'd want Phoebe with me again.

No one replied to the bell. When I peered through a glass hexagon into the attached garage, I saw no cars. Taped boxes stood heaped to the ceiling. I wondered about Phoebe's piano trophies, if she'd kept or trashed them, all those gilded, first-place spoils. Once, I'd made the mistake of asking if her father had also insisted she keep playing. He didn't attend a single re-cital, she said. Then, considering, she added, Maybe he wanted to, though. It's possible he just wasn't invited. I wouldn't have cared, not at the time.

I slid down, hitting sloped concrete, and then I crawled around to the side of the house, where I'd be less in sight. I didn't think it was legal, being here. Ivied leaves starred a white lat-tice. Noticing a scrap beneath a wilted stalk, torn hazard tape, I picked it up. I spat on it, then rubbed it clean. Thin plastic rip-pled to the touch. I sat against the wall.

The day the rest of Jejah's warrants were issued, Jo Hilt had been located in a private hospital in Lott, Connecticut, receiving in-patient psychiatric care. She released a brief written state-ment: hoping, she said, to give what answers she could. I'd have predicted that, as he tightened control of his disciples, John Leal would have introduced the idea of public violence. I knew, too, how he'd have convinced them. Privileged childhoods, the life-long habit of achieving: all the shared Jejah attributes others have found baffling would have helped him instill the bravado to do what God, in His slow-moving wisdom, had not.

But Jo claimed it was Phoebe who'd first raised questions about Phipps clinic. In the spring, she'd begun asking if they shouldn't be doing more. Local clinic protests had declined in size. Every few minutes, children died. If they could, for in-stance, disable abortion facilities, the action would save lives. It would be the rational extension of what they believed. Since no one but John Leal had spoken, to date, with God, Phoebe asked if he'd take the question to Him. Jo didn't think he would: in general, he'd told them what to do, not the reverse.

Jo hadn't learned what happened next. In mid-April, Jo's parents, Sybil and Elijah Hilt, had realized that, despite the large allowance she received each month, Jo had drawn extra funds from her trust. Disturbed, suspecting drugs, they drove up to school. While questioning Jo, Sybil had noticed whip marks on the girl's leg. They disregarded all attempts to explain; against Jo's will, they'd taken her home, to Darien. She cut her wrists, then was hospitalized.

John Leal had rented the upstate cabin to use as a spiritual retreat, starting in June, Jo said. They'd all given their savings to Jejah. Phoebe supplied the most—everything she had, as

John Leal pointed out. By then, the group comprised six members, including Eric Cho, the newest recruit. Jo had left the cult before they started using the cabin, but if I tried, I could almost see the place in June. Birch branches gleaming white, like picked bones. They lit bonfires until the sweat flowed into tears. The light tinged the circling trees with blood. They fasted, atoned. Tired bodies ached with hope. Through a haze of smoke, stars smeared like souls fleeing this fallen earth. The night chill pricked Phoebe's bare arms, as if with pinfeathers, and she felt the rush of flight, lifting up. In that isolated place, the plausible might crack open until she had the revelation she desired, a final, ecstatic fit—

But no, she wasn't the kind to have visions, no more than I'd been. I thought of what she'd said that last night, about acting as if she believed. From the start to the finish, Phoebe's want of Christ had been based in logic. She wished upon God's attested promises: the dead alive, a past repealed. This flawed world would pass, yielding to a place of undivided light. Since she lacked real belief, she might have resolved to match His pledge with action, proving the faith she craved.

Then, in the final instant, she'd have required but a little hope, a short leap of faith. Soldiers require months of training, years, before they're fit to battle, while all Phoebe had to do was put a truck in a parking lot. Several minutes' conviction, and the building falls.

I wondered when they'd learned how much had gone wrong. In Phoebe's note, she said she watched Phipps clinic collapse. Truck bombs placed, timers set, the others could have made it back to Noxhurst. They reunited on an Edwards rooftop, then opened the wine bottles. He'd have relished the call to celebrate. The building exploded. If they also noticed the whirling lights, police cars rushing toward the site, they wouldn't have thought much of it. That night, they might have driven upstate; exhausted, they slept well. It wasn't until the next morning that they'd have jumped from bed, running to the television.

Where's the—

I have it.

There! Stop!

While they watched, they fell quiet. What girls?

It's Phipps.

Phoebe then hid with them in the cabin. If Jo's right, *if*, she lived with the added guilt of having proposed the idea. But no, in fact, the more I've thought about it, Phoebe wouldn't have disputed John Leal's approach to the clinic, not in front of his group. She valued tact. If she wanted to question him, she could have pulled him aside, in private. Docile so long, she'd have been more pliant, not less.

No. He told Phoebe to bring up the idea to Jejah. With his impresario's instincts, he staged God's approval of his plan. She followed his script, but she didn't like lying. In time, she doubted his use of tricks, what such deceit implied. It was why she looked at the camera. In defiance. No one else was so rash. It was Phoebe's last, deliberate tie, to preclude turning back. I believe, Lord, help Thou mine unbelief: the skeptic's usual plea.

He'd have tried to console them. Several deaths, he said, versus the thousands killed before 5:00 each night, and that's just here, in this one failing nation. God's will. Spilt milk. She strained to accept his logic, but she wouldn't have been able to stop thinking of the five girls, the juvenile bodies blown free of an explosion, floating in pieces to the shingled cabin. Handprints glinting on bathroom glass, a hint of charred flesh: flickering at the edge of sight, these hostile children filled Phoebe's dreams.

When she learned she was the principal suspect, Phoebe might have been relieved. It was an excuse to leave; it would help the group if she could be apart from them. She left without telling anyone, driving south. Still upstate, she paused to post the note to me. If it's true, as has been reported, that the others have since slipped through Montreal, then Jejah long ago obtained false passports for everyone, including Phoebe. They had the funds. She kept driving: into Mexico, perhaps. From there, in disguise, she might have taken a plane. She could be anywhere.

I'd last heard from Fitz a week ago, before I decided to go to L.A. In the news, I'd been identified as Phoebe Lin's old boyfriend; since then, I had reporters calling, along with patriots who wished me dead, in jail. Shot. Praised. So, when a restricted number flashed on my phone, I put it down. It rang again. It wasn't until the fourth call that I answered.

It's Agent Fitz, she said.

I'm hanging up.

You don't want to do that. I have news for you.

I was in Norton Hall, going to class. Swerving left, I went into a single-person bathroom. I locked myself in. You had that footage when you talked to me, didn't you? I said. With Phoebe. The tape. You lied to get me to tell—

Don't be a child. You knew what I was doing. If you didn't, you're a fool. I'm calling because I said I'd help find Phoebe, and I hold up my end of a promise. It'll be out before long, but I wanted to tell you ahead of time.

Fitz said that a man, a Noxhurst local, had been jogging down the Hudson. It was as he approached Hoyt Bridge that he glimpsed the long hair he'd seen in photos, a blue dress, falling from the rail. But Phoebe didn't own blue clothing. She thought it washed out her skin. He didn't see a face, so it might have been anyone. It could have been nothing at all: a flock of black-pinioned birds, flicking mid-flight, like a ponytail. The feathers shredding trapezoids of blue into the trick lines of a girl's dress. Less than a mile from the clinic, he'd have had the attacks in mind. I let Fitz persist, talking, until she admitted they'd failed to find the alleged suicide's body.

Based on evidence I can't disclose, she said, the bureau has concluded the man did, in fact, see Phoebe fall from a bridge.

She sent you a note we had to intercept: I can't give it to you, but I'll make sure its contents are passed along.

I have to go, I said.

I switched off my phone; I laughed until I couldn't breathe. That evening, I had received an email from Fitz, the note digitized, then attached.

> I watched from the roof while God's hand flattened the killing mill. I thought I'd see the face of God and live. Will, I've since learned that it's possible to love life without loving mine.

I left the house; I drove around. I returned to the church, then again to his house. But I found no sign of him. I passed the light-glossed billboards. In this hot, sun-blanched limbo, I circled back and forth between his house and church until I fell asleep in the front seat. The next morning, the church parking lot sparkled with cars, packed in lines, like sheaved fish. I'd arrived in the middle of a service. I found a stall in front of the church, with a woman sitting behind the table. She smiled as I walked up, but when I asked if Reverend Lin was preaching, she said no.

Is he leading services this week?

No.

When will he be here?

He is having break, she said.

I went to the airport. The flight I'd scheduled would have taken me straight back to Noxhurst, so I changed the ticket, routing it through San Francisco. I waited to call until I was on my mother's front stoop. The phone rang from behind the fence. When I said where I was, she rushed out, still in gloves. She wiped her eyes, brushing soil on pale skin. I tried to lighten the mood: I asked if she was in the habit of gardening with a phone in hand.

Oh, this, she said. I can't hear the phone ring from the yard, and I don't like to miss it when you call. What a surprise. I'm so glad. Let's go inside.

———

But do I have it wrong, Phoebe: did you act in faith, not doubt, the clinic bomb a tribute to the God you loved? I'll say this: I hope so. If I can't imagine you lit with His fire, it's possible I'm limited, not you. In the apartment, when I left, I discovered the kidskin journal in which you took notes before Jejah confessions, jotting down what you'd tell them, us. It was stashed behind a pile of books, where Fitz and Hugh, of course, had searched. Soft-leathered, tied with a thong strip, it has the look of a journal. Yet they missed it, a bit of grace I can't explain. I've imagined as I could. I compile what I have of you, parts of it firsthand; the rest, inferred. Details accrue, taking on a living shape. I fill in the clues. I recall what John Leal said, how his shining lies persuaded you. I can't forget what you said, that I hadn't even tried to understand. Phoebe, I still don't think He's real. I believe that we, in the attempt to live, invented Him. But if I could, I'd ask Him to give you everything.

If you did jump, though. I used to preach that God holds us on a lightweight leash that will stretch to span the miles and years. We imagine ourselves free, but with a flick of His wrist He'll bring us back to Him again. It takes less than I used to think from this hope of reunion that it's not, from what I can tell, the truth. I think of the hours you spent in that Olympic pool. You'd turned so strong. Muscle-built. The Hudson, at Hoyt Bridge, isn't wide. It might have been cold, but not past surviving. It would be such an artful ruse, Phoebe, if this is how you'll elude pursuit: in having pretended to die.

The months flashed past, into a final Edwards term. I found a roommate, Bilal. He slept in the living room, behind a partition. I told Leigh I should stop wasting her time. Though I avoided the clinic site, I noticed an article about plans to build an office plaza. I thought, at times, I heard the distant drills, reveilles beating like a pulse. I wasn't sleeping much, but I threw out the pills; I tried to drink less, living to prove I'd changed.

I graduated, then I moved to Manhattan. I began a job, a full-time position at the previous summer's hedge fund. One June morning, as I walked to the train station, I saw Julian. I was lost in thought; by the time I recognized him, he'd passed in front of me, his bulk constrained in a light suit, striding in the opposite direction.

Julian, I said. I thought I saw him flinch, but he didn't respond. He'd have kept walking if I hadn't said it again, taking his arm. Julian, hello, I said, but the face he showed me might have been a stranger's. He had on glasses. The reflected sunlight hid his eyes. He looked down at the hand I'd put on his arm, and I lifted it.

I want nothing to do with you, he said. I know what you are, Will.

I don't understand.

With his glasses leveled at me like lights, he said Phoebe had told him what I'd done. That girl, he said. She'd refused to listen to him. He'd urged Phoebe to go to the police, but she didn't want to hurt me. In his frustration, he'd said things he regretted. They hadn't talked since. She'd loved me. It made little sense to him, but she had. I'd given Phoebe the last push into Jejah. He hoped I realized that. Oh, he'd fantasized about exposing me, but at least I had to keep living in my own skin: a hell, he said, he'd wish upon no one else.

They still haven't found Jejah. Once in a while, a politician promises they'll be located. In principle, the manhunt continues. The absence of proof, I've come to believe, isn't proof on its own. I've noticed signs, each of which might be incidental, but not like this, as a whole, collected. I've received phone calls that hang up at the first ring; a mailed brochure to a concert-hall Libich revival. Then, not long ago, I left the office to get lunch at Meilai's, a third-story Sichuan dive I liked. I was in line when I glanced toward the street. I saw Phoebe, in a striped sundress, looking up from the shade of an ailanthus. She'd lost weight, hair cut short; still, it was Phoebe. She turned, shoulders jutting out. I ran down. I shouted, but she'd gone. I'm aware of what people are saying, that she's drowned, lost, but I also know Phoebe. I'll open the door to a ringing bell, and she'll be there: short-haired, face split open with a smile. You don't even look surprised, she'll tell me.

That morning in June, when I'd seen Julian, I went down into the Columbus Circle station. It was loud inside, the platform more crowded than usual. I sighted the source of the tumult: a band of six male dancers, in white latex tights. With bodies liberated from gravity's laws, they swung out of handsprings into lithe spins. More people turned to watch while an express train hurtled in, the gust of wind nudging thin fabric around bare arms and thighs. The wind blew through, until it looked as if the entire population might float up out of the tunnel, cracking through its stone and earth, into the day's hot light. We can all go. No one gets left behind. The world's graves fling open, the giddied, dirt-stained dead rushing toward the streets of gold, alive again, at last.

The wind settled. In minutes, the local train arrived. I pushed in, then I kept waiting.

ACKNOWLEDGMENTS

With profound gratitude to Ellen Levine, agent extraordinaire, and to Martha Wydysh and Alexa Stark. To Laura Perciasepe, best of editors. To Glory Anne Plata and Jennifer Huang, splendid publicists, and to the rest of wonderful Riverhead, especially Janice Kurzius, Jennifer Eck, Melissa Solis, Mia Alberro, Lucia Bernard, Claire Vaccaro, Jaya Miceli, Helen Yentus, Katie Freeman, Jynne Dilling Martin, Carla Bruce-Eddings, Bob Belmont, Wendy Pearl, Brian Etling, and Brian Contine.

To the National Endowment for the Arts, the MacDowell Colony, the Bread Loaf Writers' Conference, the Sewanee Writers' Conference, the Steinbeck Fellowship, Omi International, the Norman Mailer Writers Colony, the Elizabeth George Foundation, the Squaw Valley Writers Workshops, the Napa Valley Writers'

Conference, Hedgebrook, the Anderson Center, and the Creative Capacity Fund, for vital support. To the Corporation of Yaddo, for the remarkable generosity of three fellowships.

To Michael Cunningham, my mentor all these years. To Jenny Offill, Joshua Henkin, Ernesto Mestre, Catherine Texier, Stacey D'Erasmo, Sheila Kohler, André Aciman, Christine Schutt, Peter Ho Davies, Charles Baxter, Amy Bloom, John Crowley, Katharine Weber, and Jennifer Kennedy, my inimitable teachers.

To Tony Tulathimutte, Laura van den Berg, Vauhini Vara, Andi Winnette, Anthony Ha, Vanessa Janowski, Raja Haddad, Cristina Moracho, M. A. Taft-McPhee, and M. Brett Smith, admired friends who read drafts of this book. To my esteemed writing group, past and present, including Colin Winnette, Daniel Levin Becker, Esmé Weijun Wang, Rachel Khong, Alice Sola Kim, Anisse Gross, Karan Mahajan, Caille Millner, Katrina Dodson, Pola Oloixarac, Jennifer duBois, Annie Julia Wyman, Katherine Marino, Lydia David Fitzpatrick, Diane Cook, and Greg Larson. To my Brooklyn College cohort, especially Andy Hunter, Hugh Merwin, Robert Jones, and Scott Lindenbaum, who saw *The Incendiaries* at its start.

To friends whose advice, help, and encouragement sustained me: Vanessa Hua, Bich Minh Nguyen, Kirstin Chen, Aimee Phan, Frances Hwang, Marie Mutsuki Mockett, Garnette Cadogan, Alexander Chee, Lauren Groff, Viet Thanh Nguyen, Celeste Ng, Rabih Alameddine, Josh Weil, Christine Hyung-Oak Lee, Nayomi Munaweera, Yalitza Ferreras, Cara Bayles, Matthew Salesses, Carmen Maria Machado, Peter Mountford, Alexi Zentner, Michael David Lukas, Ross White, Matthew Olzmann, James Scott, Susan Steinberg, Elliott Holt, Marie-Helene Bertino, Chloe Benjamin, Rebecca Makkai, Thomas Meaney, Cara Blue Adams, Mike Scalise, Dara Barnat, Gerald Maa, Lawrence-Minh Bùi Davis, Sonya Larson, Shuchi Saraswat, Harriet Clark, Jennine Capó Crucet, Elena Passarello, Hasanthika Sirisena, Dave Lucas, Tomás Q. Morín, Michael Croley, Giuseppe Taurino, Nina McConigley, Xhenet Aliu, Ru Freeman, Sarah Gerkensmeyer, Chloe Honum, Amanda Goldblatt, Luis Jaramillo, David James Poissant, Julie Iromuanya, Anne Valente, Seth Tucker, Rebecca Makkai, Kyle Minor, Mary Kim-Arnold, Michelle Hoover, Kirstin Valdez Quade, Krys Lee, Vikram Chandra, CJ Hauser, Marie Myung-Ok Lee, Christian Kiefer, Lydia Kiesling, Nicole Chung, Ingrid Rojas Contreras, Crystal Kim, Lillian Li, Danielle Lazarin, Adrienne Celt, Aja Gabel, Rachel Lyon, Tracy O'Neill, Patricia Park, James Cañón, Brandon Hobson, Piyali Bhattacharya, Anna Keesey, Oscar Villalon, Julie Buntin, Colin Drohan, Garth Greenwell, and Lucy Tan.

To Emily Ballaine, Stephen Sparks, Molly Parent, Brad Johnson, Vanessa Martini, Paul Yamazaki, and Dan Weiss, for recommendations and camaraderie.

To Diane Williams, and to *Noon*, where short excerpts of *The Incendiaries* first appeared in slightly different form; to Madelaine Lucas, Rebekah Bergman, Zach Davidson, Hilary Leichter, Rita

Bullwinkel, and Emily Tobin. To Stuart Dybek and Tara Masih, who selected an excerpt for *The Best Small Fictions*. To Thomas Ross, and to *Tin House*, where an excerpt appeared.

To John Kwon, Christine Ji Min Kwon, Lynn Dawson, Carl Dawson, Karen Occhipinti, and Vince Occhipinti, always. To the examples set forth by Agnes Shin, Chang Ho Shin, Byung Rim Kwon, and Tae Ryong Kwon. To Clara Kwon and Young Kwon, for everything.

To Michael, first reader, my love, who believed even when I couldn't.